THE PANIPURI CRIMES

THE PANIPURI CRIMES

S B AKSHOBHYA

Srishti
PUBLISHERS & DISTRIBUTORS

Srishti Publishers & Distributors
A unit of AJR Publishing LLP
212A, Peacock Lane
Shahpur Jat, New Delhi – 110 049
editorial@srishtipublishers.com

First published by
Srishti Publishers & Distributors in 2021

10 9 8 7 6 5 4 3 2 1

To my wife
Chandrika,
The first reader of all my scripts,
Especially the ones inscribed in the heart.

Contents

Acknowledgement

"*Kathe,*" the one-word every night request from my daughter Pranathi asking for a bedtime story over the past decade must have invoked my grey cells towards the realm of fiction writing. I don't have any other explanation why I would have deviated from the technical track of writing books on Statistics, Machine Learning, R and Python to an out-and-out thriller.

My parents have been voracious readers themselves. I have seen my mother Lakshmi read many Kannada and Telugu novels as a kid, and my father Narayanachar has a long quest to understand the truth in sacrilegious texts.

Working with my editor Stuti has been a pleasure, and the manuscript in your hand has benefited with the crisp work by team Srishti Publishers. I also thank Arup Bose for bringing the novel into your hands.

Shivram K has provided a lot of literary stimulus and our colloquy helped us traverse the infinite universe of fiction.

Finally, I would like to thank you, the reader, for picking up this book. Welcome to the world of panipuri crimes and congratulations on completing the first set of steps in the 'vibes world'.

1 Sagar's Limits

Obsession went for a drive on the highway whenever Sagar Bansal hit the local panipuri stall. "Sagar's limits, ha, ha," Sagar's mentee Rudra laughed.

'Sagar's limits' sounded ironic because the name Sagar meant the sea; and the commonly perceived belief is that a sea has no limit. Sagar's appetite for panipuri was as infinite as the ocean. He was already munching on the seventeenth one.

"Isn't it better to have panipuri rather than a cigarette?" Sagar mocked his buddy who had paused for a smoke amid their no-prize competition of eating the most number of panipuris.

"The cocaine helps to overcome the stress," Rudra answered.

"I have much more stress than you," Sagar said. The panipuri vendor Alok had paused for further instructions after serving the eighteenth puri, so Sagar turned to him, "Bring it on! Today I am more worn out than this smoker Rudra." The tension was undoubtedly palpable on his face.

"*Tikha lagaun*?" asked Alok. He needed to know how spicy Sagar wanted it.

"*Haan, tikha*," nodded Sagar. On cue, Alok stirred the pot again and sprinkled additional pinches of chilli powder over the mashed potato. Sagar took two drags from Rudra's smoking barrel. "You were right about doing the research before getting serious with this smirky business of my soul's favourite. That's giving me the blues whether I should indulge in it or not," Sagar expressed his concern.

"What did it reveal to make you worry so much?" Rudra enquired.

"All the five entrepreneurs who tried their hand at selling this damn thing online have died in accidents," Sagar said. The summary made Rudra shiver.

"You can't mean it," Rudra said in disbelief.

"Come, I will tell you over drinks!" added Sagar and finally put his plate down.

An ardent aficionado of the panipuri, Sagar felt if he was destined to go the entrepreneur way, it had to be through the online sales of panipuri. He drafted his approach and was mightily pleased with his efforts. To Sagar's utter shock, the five aspirants who had earlier floated the idea of venturing into the online sales of panipuri had died in accidents, one after the other. Plus, all of them were killed in a zone not covered by any surveillance camera. They were all young, between their mid-twenties and forties. Could the attempt to sell panipuri online have led to their death? It chilled his bones. Rudra's as well.

The famous panipuri is also exultingly known by other names like *golgappa, phuchka, pakodi, paani ke patashe, gup chup, phulki, paani ke batashe, tikki*, water pancake and watery bread. Sagar felt sublime every time he visited the local vendor who would put out a vertical bamboo or cane rack with transparent polythene covering the puris. The special lime-water in the earthen pot, onion chops mildly mixed with sliced carrot, and boiled potatoes mashed with the panipuri masala was his escape to paradise from the infernal abyss named the IT world.

The obsession was not a one-sided affair; the trophies stacked in his cabinet in Hindi poetry contests were a testimony. While others in the competition rendered love, heartbreak, national issues, sports star enigma, artists, et al. in their works, judges almost always rated Sagar's narration as an ensemble of the popular poetry topics as a podium finisher. The songs praising his affair with panipuri fetched him much applause. From his high-school days in Vidisha, a major city of Madhya Pradesh, he knew nearly a dozen of his friends who impressed their girlfriends by merely replacing panipuri in his poem with the girl's name. A handful of girls had even threatened to switch to Sagar after finding out the truth. As a penance, the boys promised to sponsor one-month of panipuris for the girls and the poet.

A friend suggested the poet publish his collection of poems. As much as Sagar laughed off the idea, the first print-and-bound hundred copies sold like hot cakes beside a chaat centre. Encouraged with the instantaneous success, a local publisher in Vidisha published the compilation. The collection had never been out of print since the first print half a decade ago.

Expert, authority, thespian, scholar, specialist, doctor, sage and pandit... Sagar felt he had covered all of the superlatives in his affairs with the eatery. "You are no Einstein or Hawking. Heck, you are not APJ Kalam either. What's your contribution to the growth or sustenance of panipuri's popularity?" teased his girlfriend Rathishree. Her point was that he was a beneficiary of the panipuri, but he hadn't added anything towards the product's growth. Her provocation compelled out of the box thinking, and that led to the idea of selling the simpleton eatery online.

Two rounds of the strong beer done with, and an unknown count in the waiting, the two tango flatmates Sagar and Rudra were discussing the findings. S Mohit was the first in Sagar's research who attempted setting up the online world of these spice bombs. The other four who died in accidents were Sripathi F, Kaushik, Rodriquez M, and Anjali R. All the casualties were during the past eighteen months, and each of these young business people was three months to fourteen months into the business.

With the advantage of the first mover, Mohit reached a peak of serving fifty-thousand dishes over six months through his online portal. He had tied up with six footpath pavement vendors. As with the current trend of Zomato, Uber Eats and Swiggy of online food sales, he had set up an online portal only through his Facebook account. The network was strong enough to get him sufficient orders. In his now-frozen statement of social media, the last update read as "Big deal coming my way. Watch this space for more details." When he died in an accident in Sanjay Nagar, the corner place was not covered by CCTV surveillance.

Sripathi was thirty-six years old when he tried his hands at the brisk business of panipuri orders through e-service. His module was elementary. He simply advertised his mobile number, probably using an extra SIM for the purpose. The user had to send a message in a given format, to correspond to the number of plates. He spent close to five lakh rupees in local pamphlet distribution. It was torrential rain rendering the surveillance cameras ineffective when a truck ran over, laying him to waste at Goutami Layout.

Kaushik and Rodriquez's cases were not much different from Mohit and Sripathi. While Kaushik tried his hands at Rajarajeshwari Nagar and Rodriquez in Indira Nagar, both of them were struck under a span of three days. Kaushik tried his hand at developing a website, and Rodriquez resorted mainly to social media for customer traction. The latter even got a second-string Malayalam television artist to endorse his business. Rudra dismissed Sagar's apprehensions by pointing out that while Rodriquez died in an accident in Whitefield, Kaushik's body was found on a railway track, indicating the possibility of a suicide.

The last case was surprising. Anjali turned out to be a colleague of Sagar as both of them were working in the renowned multinational software company, Accenture. However, Sagar was not aware of her until the day of his research. Curiously, Anjali being forty-three years old and in the HR team, had access to the big shots of the entrepreneur universe. She was an agonising four-days shy of signing with a venture capitalist for one-hundred and fifty thousand dollars worth of seed funding.

"Why don't you try connecting with a common friend? I mean, even though she is deceased, you are bound to find a common connection in our company who can tell you more," Rudra suggested.

"That's the benefit of sitting with a drinking buddy. Cheers!" saying that, Sagar quickly launched a check on the LinkedIn professional platform. He knew Dhruv, who was closely connected with Anjali. Sagar wasted no time in reaching out to Dhruv.

"Hi Sagar, long time," Dhruv was delighted to get an old buddy on call.

"Hi Dhruv, how are you, mate?" Sagar was glad on being recollected easily by Dhruv. A few minutes into the conversation, he asked, "Hey, sorry buddy. I need to ask you a few questions about Anjali. I am aware that she is no more. Can you please tell me something about her?"

Dhruv admitted to being shocked over the demise of his senior manager Anjali. The deceased was a warm lady, always smiling. A caring lady who catered to almost all the requirements of her team, she had made considerable strides in her small side-business of the panipuri world. He described her fondly. Sagar had been listening keenly and threw in his suspicion that the death was more than an accident. Dhruv dismissed it on the grounds that the accident was a freefall on the long stairs from the sixteenth to the fourteenth floor. A suspected slip in the high heels led to her death, and the postmortem report confirmed the same.

The girlfriends were all away in their hometown, thanks to the extended weekend. With the data and details of the five accidents, Sagar was perplexed about whether he should try his hands and go ahead with the project, ignoring the danger. The heart wanted to go all the way in the e-panipuri world; the brain suspected a whale in the smudgy waters. Rudra's assurance did not help him conclude in either direction, and he expressed his indecisiveness. While they were discussing it after returning from office on Monday, they felt they would be better off consulting their third flatmate, Jim.

"Before Jim returns tonight, I can engage the local panipuri boy, Alok. What do you say?" Sagar told Rudra.

"Hmm, so that theory of the panipuri mafia is still lurking in your mind, isn't it?" Rudra wondered.

"Yup, you got it," Sagar asserted.

A wild panipuri mafia theory floated from the crime world. In many major cities, the local cane panipuri vendors are spread out more densely than the police check-posts. They do a roaring business, and a mobile panipuri cane set-up is found at every corner, like mosquitoes. The wild theory is that at most two or three mafias control the majority of these small sellers. The city is divided into regions by them, and irrevocably the seller on the street is a lad from either Uttar Pradesh, Bihar, Jharkhand or Uttarakhand. The typical age of the seller is between fifteen and thirty-five. Invigorating sales mean a profit of nearly a thousand rupees a day. Spread out over the five hundred such sellers in a vital city amounts to a neat profit of five lakh rupees per day, and one-and-a-half crore a month. The seller is a kind of a hostage with a payment of a paltry hundred rupees a day. A conventional mobile handset with minimum currency is given to the seller. His family in the native state is controlled by the network of the mafia in those states. Monthly maintenance of two-three thousand is thrown to the family too. In the uneventful case of the seller absconding from the city, the family is forever silenced in the home town. Was this mafia behind the five accidents?

Sagar and Rudra were at Alok's stall after ten minutes of agreeing to figure out the theory. The trick, according to Rudra, was to eat the chaat in the usual way and ask him questions. Another suggestion of Rudra that helped in getting answers from the boy was for Sagar to wear a forlorn look of a dejected lover. Alok broke impromptu while serving the second puri.

"*Saab, aap dukhi achhe nahi lagte*," Alok asked his number one customer why he looked so sad.

"Yes, Alok, that's true. My dream is shattered. I was planning to create a mobile app which will help me and your other customers to buy panipuri from you, the way Zomato, Swiggy, and Uber Eats are serving famous hotels. You know Zomato, don't you?" asked Sagar.

"Who does not know about them, sir. Is it possible, sir? Can you get me sales too?" Alok was wondering about the possibility.

"*Kyun nahi!* See, I can't come to your stall every time I have the urge, can I? Imagine if I can place an online order to fetch me five plates of panipuri from Alok?" Sagar tried to seduce him with possibilities.

"Then why don't you do it? You are an engineer and a great tech-savvy guy. You can build an app like Zomato, Uber Eats, etc. It will help people to buy panipuri from Alok within the confines of their home," Rudra set the required provocation.

"Can you do it, sir?" Alok was happy with the prospect.

With the confidence of the boy in their pockets, Sagar and Rudra revealed the details of the five accidents and how the underworld mafia controls the typical cane set-up, and panipuri boys. It took them five rounds of panipuri to complete the narration and finally, Sagar asked the boy his honest opinion.

"*Saheb, jahan darr hota hai, wahan hum nahi hote*," Alok was clear. He wanted to steer away from all of these adventures.

On their stroll back to the flat, Rudra took the deliberation as a perilous game, and Sagar was delighted all the same. According to Sagar, the danger was not the problem; it was the misconception that there might be a hazard that was even more ominous.

"What do you mean?" asked Rudra.

"See, I was thinking about going for a hunt in the wild forest. Now, the problem was with the preparation, wasn't it? The rumour of a lion in the jungle is different from the confirmation that he is ruling the roost. We know the essential tools now. Replacing the lion to take the kingdom is much easier than assembling all creatures in the wild. That would have been more dogmatic than being difficult," Sagar had the required clarity, and he decided to dab into the adventure. His belief was complimented with Jim's insight that if nobody is suspecting foul play in an accidental death, the deaths are more unexpected than being a murder.

"You son of a whore, the spit of a cobra you must be! Just wait until I am done with the next call," the fat, old rogue turned the heat on Shikhan. The twenty-four-year-old Shikhan should have been able to handle the mess of a nearly-sixty-year-old Jaani. But not in the pitch dark of midnight. When Jaani unleashed the crowbar a dozen times on the arms and thighs of Shikhan, the question of rebellion did not rise. Jaani would anyway use his crowbar at least five times a week on the hapless panipuri boys for no reason whatsoever.

The trick in catching financial irregularity is to turn a blind eye on the first occurrence. Jaani had observed the hundred rupee-galloping by Shikhan two weeks ago and intentionally let it pass. Predictable as the sunrise, the bills were perfect on the second day. The third day saw Shikhan under-report the sales by a hundred and fifty rupees. The fourth day was again perfect, and Jaani let it pass by over two weeks and lulled the boy into complacency. The eighth time Shikhan made a mistake, the cause of the scam was unearthed by Jaani using the regular local arrack. Jaani was aghast that he would have to now go the distance and unleash hell on the unsuspecting Shikhan.

Alok, Barfi, Shikhan, Jarokh, Bholu and Ghumroo shared the cramped single room home in the ghettos of Wadarabandyapalya. The six men aged between seventeen and twenty-nine made the same panipuri sales on the mobile cane set-up. The home, if ever a stinking place can be called as one, was an eight feet by ten feet hole. They slept, jammed together like sardines. The ten feet by three feet balcony would serve to host the six cane mobile shops, and it was protected by a criss-cross iron bar gate. The bathroom cum lavatory was shared by nearly twenty men in the neighbourhood. Jaani's rules were strict, and shaving was mandatory. However, not more than one person could shave on a single day, and Sunday would be a rest day for the razor. Skipping was not an option granted by the ruthless barbarian. Once a month, local arrack would be arranged, and nobody was allowed to drink until the next arrangement. Mutton biryani would accompany the drinking, and every weekend, the sellers would be entertained with a bread omelette.

The vendors were tracked on the field. The customers could be informants to Jaani, or the unseen lord of them all Baja could take any mystical form and trace them. Jaani, the informers and Baja collectively had absolute control over the footman seller. More importantly, each of them had a family who would be wiped out, root and stem, for betrayal. The rumours heard by Sagar and the commoners were surreal. The only difference was that the seller's life was a living nightmare in the pits of hell, and the dread was excruciatingly palpable.

Shikhan committed the cardinal sin on the one hundred and seventy-eighth day of being inducted into the program. On the fourteenth day of the first blasphemy, he was under the impression that his smartness had fooled the great Jaani and the higher-ups. He smirked inwardly, thinking that he had duped the system.

"Kishen, Rupesh, Javed and Rampu. Who remembers them?" Jaani asked his audience with the dawn two hours away. Alok, Barfi, Jarokh, Bholu and Ghumroo were shaken, while Shikhan, the recent inductee in the group, did not know those names. While the five of them knew that one of the six of them was in deep trouble, the moron peeled a *gutkha* sachet and welcomed it between his teeth and lower lip. The scammer had no clue of the quantum of punishment.

"Who were they, Shikhan?" asked Jaani more directly. The fool expressed his ignorance, his mouth filled with the gutkha. A resounding slap across the chin splashed the gutkha syrup on the wall. "Clean it up, you bastard!" Jaani ordered, and Shikhan promptly followed the dictum. "Six times you thought the cheap gutkha odour will hide the fragrance, didn't you?" and now the guilty realized his folly had been caught long ago.

"*Maafi, mai-baap, maafi*. Give me a final chance, please," Shikhan broke down into tears and fell at the feet of his high lord.

"Not in my hands." Jaani dialled a number reaching out to Baja, explained the guilt, and the trial was announced. Shikhan's family would be spared of the ignominy of being wiped out of the planet. Shikhan was not so fortunate.

"Mai-baap, maafi," Shikhan pleaded one more time.

"Do you know what happened with those four assholes? The crowbar got in their assholes," Jaani's voice had no remorse in expressing death. "Shut his mouth," was all Jaani said before life was squeezed out of the hapless Shikhan over the next two minutes. The body was dumped in a gunny bag by Jarokh and Bholu and then in the vehicle which was later driven away by Jaani.

Alok was confused whether he was supposed to reveal to his masters the deliberations with Sagar and Rudra. He had a hunch that those two were unrelated to this crime world. Six years in the service, he was sure he had not committed any folly and mentioning the small chatter felt needless. When the footmen sellers passed such information to the masters, more often, they were more distrusted than the suspect audience from the world. It meant their own neck was on the line. The masters were ever suspicious of the footmen sellers, and often reluctant to identify chinks in their armour. The master's solution was simple – kill them and be done away with the menace. Though the Jaanis could be reached, the Bajas were invincible. But why did he have to worry about the Shikhans, Sagars or the Jaanis? He had the more pressing problem at hand, to wake up and reach his designated post the next morning.

The website www.pp.com was obviously meant for the fans of panipuri. A fan-based forum allowed the user to create threads on any topic under the sun so long as it could be tied to a puri. The eight-year-old website was anonymously run on a server based in Russia. Panipuri lovers greeted each other by a variety of titles: Purian, Paanipurian, PPian, peeps, PP, Golgappaian, Phuchkawala, Pakodikar, etc. Apart from people using their own names as user ID, it was common to tweak the ID with prefixes or suffixes with trendy extensions: 007, BOSS, Potter, Harry, Om, Modi, Shah, Singh, Roger, Djokovic, Nadal, SPB, 101, BigBang, Bookman, etc.

A recent star user of the online forum turned out to be Liliana. This user, apart from being a panipuri fanatic, turned out to have the coolest photo ID, swag and was very flirtatious towards the men on the forum. She would not be on the forum for more than fifteen minutes a day, and yet her arrival was anticipated in every internet byte spent on the website. Her profile showed her as a nineteen-year-old residing in Pakodi Apartment, Phuchka City, Chats State and Tikki Country. The profile was obviously a fake one, and nobody gave a damn. All Liliana had to do was create a new thread and simply say 'Hi!' and it would attract a few hundred likes and seventy to eighty comments. Liliana had put on a hell of a profile and gave away much gyan on the variants of panipuri.

"The Master Chef's Guide to Panipuri ," "Seven Most Popular PP Variants," "50 Shades of Water Pancakes," "Vanilla PP is the best PP," "Roger Federer likes Golgappas," "The Unhygienic PP," etc., gave a snippet of the discussions that happened on www.pp.com.

2 The Vibes Ventures

Sagar, Rudra and Jim – the three eligible bachelors – had gorgeous girlfriends in Rathishree, Yashashwini and Koyal. The sextet occupied Flat 1304 in Greenville Apartments, HSR Layout. The boys might play the game of eating more panipuris exceedingly well, but even then, they were no match in besting the count of eating the panipuris when the girls took the field. Only Rathishree was the loser among girls because even with the gender advantage, she was not able to beat Sagar. However, the girls ended up as the overall winners by the permanent score of 2-1. The cosmopolitan city reflected the diversity of the country, and the close buddies' group too. Sagar Bansal hailed from the central Indian state of Madhya Pradesh, Rudra was a localite, and Jim was from Kerala. Religion was not a consideration among the friends, and it reflected in their outreach too. Rathishree, Yashashwini and Koyal were from Karnataka, Maharashtra and Uttar Pradesh, respectively.

Friday evening was an early return to the nest for the three couples. The cook was specific in his contract that he wouldn't work from Friday evening to Sunday evening. The busy hours over the weekend meant quick money, and he did not want to give leverage to the cheaper tariff averaged over the monthly bulk fees. After a knock on each door asking for the preferred choice of food, the usual consensus boiled down to pizzas. The family pack of two large pizzas from Domino's had enough slices for the six of them. Rudra made the enquiry on every demanding Friday evening, playing the role as precisely as possible.

Kingfisher Strong beer was stocked in abundance, and two dozen cans were easily washed down by the end of the weekend. The delivery boy rang the bell at nine 9.42 p.m. and handed over the non-veg burger pizza topped with chicken salami and a corn-cheese-mushroom veg pizza. The Pepsis were ordered separately, and the six vicenarians stormed the dining table at ten when they could not resist the tantalizing aroma filling their bedrooms.

"Yummy, I just love chicken salami-burger pizza," Koyal could chomp her way to the last bite on the table.

"If there was an award for the perfect order accumulator, it'd go to Rudra," grinned Sagar.

"You just need to find an excuse to praise your prodigy, isn't it?" smirked Rathishree.

"Don't be salty on Friday night, please," Jim asked for a refrain.

"That's fine. Is the order to your satisfaction, Rathi?" enquired Rudra.

"For the hundredth time, Rudra, I have begged you not to cut my name short. Yet, our friends blame only me for the friction," Rathishree could not hide her disappointment.

"Are you fine with the order, Rathishree?" Rudra politely reiterated his question.

Rathishree took her share of two slices from the veg pizza and using the fork, she picked out the mushrooms on the dining mat. She did not have to say it explicitly, and it might have been the fourth time in as many months that it escaped her ex-boyfriend's memory that his Rathi was the same Rathishree who abhorred mushrooms and everything that is non-vegetarian. Yashashwini indicated to her boyfriend Rudra that she did not appreciate. It was the charisma of Sagar Bansal that gelled the six youngsters, and it was for his sake that the quadrilateral of conflicts, including himself, Rathishree, Rudra and Yashashwini, lived under the same roof. The current formation was not aged six months for that matter.

Sagar Bansal was a masterful tactician, and because of his virtue, the six not-so-great earners could afford living in the exquisite apartment. Two years ago, he formed an alliance with Jim and Rudra who were rank freshers with a not-so-big freshers' salary pack. A proud alumnus of BITS Pilani, he tracked his immediate juniors, and when they graduated, he offered them residence at the plush HSR Layout. The quantum of rent was manageable when six purses came together to share the burden. Would they be able to get a foot inside the grand apartment complex, let alone something so significant as Greenville where anybody with the status less than a CTO, Director or CEO would be shunned? Sagar tailed another highly successful Bansal entrepreneur and managed to get hold of the million-dollar earner flat at 1304. When the richer and more experienced engineer got a three-year VISA and full-time role in Los Angeles, Sagar coerced and convinced the distant relative into reneging his lease amount. With the common Bansal name, society secretary Romila Tagore did not suspect a rat. The rent of sixty thousand a month translated to a considerable lump sum of twenty plus lakh for the other Bansal, and the current resident would get to explore the Richie-rich of the society.

"Rudra, why are you hesitating?" Sagar enquired on finding the latter sceptical about joining, almost two years ago. Jim informed him that the youngest of the three had a girlfriend, Rathishree.

"What about you?" asked Sagar. Jim had his steady girlfriend in Koyal Mehra. "The more, the merrier," Sagar announced and immediately a ladies' room was formed in one of the three bedrooms. Sagar kept the master bedroom for himself all the time. The flat very soon entertained the love birds with nests. Sagar bitched about how he was the only one without any love and yet he chose to focus on the business world, and he would always play with ideas and flaunt them on online forums and other venues. Blogs, Vlogs, LinkedIn, Stackexchange, Github, and other online media kept him ever busy. His work ethic rubbed on others, and very soon, most of them were fully occupied on the weekends with innovation and creative ideas.

A three-month stint in Cologne took Rudra to Germany. A few months ago, Yashashwini joined as a new flatmate. She was handpicked by Sagar, and it showed in the received preferential treatment – the small study room was given for her exclusive use. Sagar desperately wanted the label of IIT in his more extensive scheme of things. He despised organic growth, and he had to show something massive to break through the shackles of venture funding. When Jim reflected that the only few months older Sagar had time on his side, the first illegal occupant reminded him that one is always late for entrepreneurship. Sagar was on the verge of sacrificing his master bedroom for Yashashwini when the alert and insecure Rathishree reverted to their arrangement in the flat.

Rathishree was as greedy as it takes to be successful and she realized that the new lass on the floor stood a better chance of conversion at the higher stakes by her better brand label, attractiveness and intelligence too. The stakes were getting higher, and without informing and updating her flatmates, Rathishree slowly converted her full-time work to sixty per cent workload, taking a hit in her salary. In Rudra's absence, she was not distracted by the lack of intimacy. She spared four days of a week on Sagar's entrepreneur ideas. The fresher Yashashwini was left miles behind in the rear mirror.

Rudra's return after three months of tenure gave rise to new complications. When he found some free time in the day with Rathi, his Rathishree, the wild on hormones understandably craved for sex, as they routinely had in the past two years. The snub was unreal and the reluctance unimaginable. There was none of his Rathi in the fierce and competitive Rathishree, and she expressed that she had an urgent deliverable over the next six hours. Rudra reluctantly withdrew. He was shocked to see Rathi engaged in a discussion with Sagar at the end of six hours.

"I thought it was your office work, Rathi," he groaned amid the brainstorming session between her and Sagar.

"Work is work, and I need to slog out my options," Rathishree was not any less accomplished than her boyfriend.

"We need to speak, Rathi," Rudra emphasised.

"Rudra, do you have to intervene amid our brainstorming?" Sagar never liked losing out on the role of being the alpha male.

"Rathi, one minute," Rudra was clear he wanted to talk to his girl and not his mentor. She was clearly displeased with his meddling in the meeting. It was a matter of discipline, if not integrity, for her. Before she could get into even more complex conventions, Sagar's nod saved her from ambiguity. She went with her boy to their bedroom.

The one-word summary of Rudra's conflict could be traced to 'ego' and he wasn't modest enough to hide it. He expressed his disappointment with her choosing work over love. "It might be a holiday for you to recoup from the jet-lag. I have no such excuse, Rudra," Rathishree explained that she could not concede the ground to the newbie Yashashwini, and she had taken a cut on her full pay-load to break through the technical implementation of Sagar's entrepreneur needs.

Rudra was aghast that she hid the salary hit affair from him. "What's that to you, Rudra?" she quipped, and he was shocked at her temerity.

"I am your love," he asserted. Rathishree calmed down and agreed to resolve the issue. She begged Sagar to be excused for two days, and she was granted the wish.

Her heart was unquestionably with Rudra, and yet her work and time moved to a large extent with Sagar's ideas. With her lack of time for him, Rudra was slipping away on his own to the siren Yashashwini. When the newbie asked for help, it was not long before Rudra found love for a second time too soon. He helped Yashashwini to switch from her company to his, and the two began commuting to the office. Unbeknownst to herself, the young and handsome Rudra was soon a seductive attraction for her, and when the guy proposed, she did not decline, fully aware of his beloved Rathi.

Rudra schemed his way to getting caught pants down. He observed that Sagar and Rathishree went out for evening snacks to Alok's chaat centre on alternate days. He loafed in the nearby garden and catching his former love approaching with Sagar, he put his hand around Yashashwini and smooched her. Rudra pretended to be shocked at being caught and retired to the apartment, faking embarrassment.

Rathishree was truly heartbroken, and could not forgive the betrayal. She did not discount the junior Yashashwini either. She had an ugly showdown with her boyfriend, and when confronted, Rudra was sure that he could not wait an eternity for her return from her never-ending work. In his attempt to put her down, he praised his new love as more beautiful and accommodative. Three days later, when the sobbing girl sat on a cement bench at the other corner of the garden, Sagar lent a shoulder to cry on. As he consoled the crying girl, their eyes locked on each other. It was uncomfortable and uneasy. Yet, it was not the first time for either of them, and they knew that they could undoubtedly find love in the other. A kiss sealed it for them, when words would have certainly been a dumb affair.

Sagar-Rathishree, Rudra-Yashashwini, and Jim-Koyal quickly took to the three nests of the flat and everything was forgiven, though not easily in the triangle affair of Rudra-Rathishree-Yashashwini.

"Pepsi, Rathishree?" Yashashwini suggested that the furious girl wash down the pizza with the carbonated drink. She had a not-so-cordial relationship with the queen of the master bedroom.

"Thanks, Yashashwini, but tell me honestly. Why do I have to make a compromise with my favourite? Why should I substitute my all-time favourite Greater Than gin with the lame carbonated drink?" Rathishree was clearly pissed off with the compromises she had to put up with.

"You have to compromise with your favourite because it is out of stock, and we are not your stockists. Sad, but that's the bottom and top of it," Yashashwini preferred to be blunt.

"I hate to add this Yashu, but I have to. Greater Than gin is not cheap and it costs a thousand bucks for three-fourths of a litre. Since the last time I had stocked it, I hadn't consumed a third of it, and I sincerely loathe telling you who sipped the rest," Rathishree was clear. It was getting serious and the next speaker had the potential to perilously vitiate the silence of the darkness.

Rathishree picked a can of the strong beer and retired to her room, absolving her audience of further uncomfortable inarticulateness. Sagar cheered the flatmates in the absence of his girlfriend. He could understand why Rathi was so fussy about Rudra and perceived her agitation. It did not help that she was needlessly marginalized by Rudra. The senior took care for the welfare of each occupant of his flat. He appreciated Rathi's maturity in not asking Rudra and Yashaswini to move out of 1304. The very same lady couldn't be labelled as jealous for expecting a few of her desires to be laid out on the dining table. A mind as stable as hers could hardly be called out as a fanatic's mind. He had to speak with her, knowing what she was really upset about.

At the meeting followed by the next day's breakfast, the more substantial roles were clearly defined. The development of the mobile app platform was the biggest challenge. The website hosting and its content were assigned to Rathi, the mobile app development to Rudra and the database and real-time technology management to Yashashwini. Social media advertisement and blog management fell into Jim and Koyal's domain. Sagar's role consisted of all the other activities. Rudra held on to the second rank overriding the contributions of the proposed website developer.

"I think you are better off by not defending me from Rathi's attacks," Rudra told Yashu when the door was resolutely locked, and the lights were off sans the bed lamp.

"The whore is jealous of you supplanting her position in Sagar's new adventure. I don't get how he puts up with that slut," Yashu bitched about a bitch. She could see through his dismay with her choice of words. "She's no less a loose mouth than a cheap whore, come on! She ruined the dinner, and you better not comply with her and spoil my night," the girl removed her jacket and tossed it in the open wardrobe.

"She's not a bad girl," Rudra added while helping her get out of the purple shirt.

"She's spread her legs wide enough to take both of you. Don't I know," Yashu was in the groove.

"I don't remember how it was with her since the time I kissed you in the garden," he tried to replicate the kiss that brought them together.

Koyal and Jim did not require an extraordinary moment for Cupid to bind them together. Pragmatic love – that was them. He was likeable, and hence she liked him. He held the same perspective. They loved food more than each other. 'No regrets' was an essential mantra for the couple, and even as the other couples of the flat were in no hurry whatsoever to settle down with one another, Koyal-Jim's parents met, and an engagement was on the cards. This couple indeed looked ahead for the marriage under a year, and obliging the bride-to-be's parents, Jim's parents were agreeeable to a Hindu marriage.

"Do you think Rudra deliberately tries to get on Rathi's nerves?" asked Koyal. The question was not out of place, and if Rudra was indeed genuine in his forgetfulness, he would be forgetting the others' favourites too, and that had never happened. More so, Yashashwini's needs were doubly taken care of, and Sagar's triply addressed. They themselves never had a shortage, even though there was not a penny of abundance.

"Yeah, I too smell a rat. I mean, why would Rudra go out of his way and finish off her gin during the working week. Rathi is barely a fussy woman, and she's been very polite and considerate in exercising her position in 1304. Who's more sound between the squabbling women?" Jim asked.

"Do you mean between Rathi and Yashu? I mean, look, the youngest member is just out of college and not even completed a year. So certainly, she lacks the experience. However, what she lacks in experience, she aggravates and spoils in her attitude. I am no expert coder, and not a novice either. And then we have two Rathis – pre-Sagar's work one and post-Sagar's work. The latter is bettered only by Sagar. In terms of attitude too, Rathi is best after her current lover. The two are such a powerhouse that no amount of branding is compensated by the barrage of excuses by Rudra and Yashu. The lad is clearly jealous that his IIT girl is not given prominence over an ordinary engineering graduate. Until now, Rudra's greatest achievement is following Sagar's footsteps. He would not have got the three months onsite travel otherwise. What do you think?" Koyal finally threw the ball in her lover's court.

"Rathi is a great asset for Sagar, until now. There is no way he could have got so much work out of anybody on a volunteer basis," Jim quipped.

"She's got rich rewards too, didn't she?" Koyal hinted at Rathi becoming Sagar's muse.

"She was driven into Sagar's arms because Rudra now wanted Yashu to be his girlfriend, isn't it?" Jim laughed at the dog-eat-dog business world.

"Sagar's a big-ticket win for Rathi. Come on, you can't deny it."

"As things stand right at the moment, Sagar's net value is nothing more than all the tangibles in his bedroom. Let's give

Rathi her due credit. It takes more than simply the will to displace Sagar's perceived favourite in Yashu as it stood in the beginning. It took a hell lot of sacrifice and effort for Rathi. What is it that you continually say about Yashu's attitude? She stinks more by relying on her beauty and premier institute label to see her through the day. Won't work in the long run, not with the likes of Sagar," Jim was more deliberate this time around.

"Where do you see yourself six months down the line?" asked Koyal.

"In you, just as now," and Jim began the deep thrusts as she too tried to match his rhythm. He winked, and she raised herself to smooch him and slash her tongue against his.

The intimate actions were missing in magnitude in the master bedroom. A deep kiss too did not take the aloofness out of Rathishree. Her disappointment was less with the dining table shortcomings of Rudra, and more with his and Jim's failure to stop Sagar in the new adventure of online sales of the panipuri. It was not that she was scared of taking risks. It was the brute physical punishment leading even to death that intimidated her. A million other avenues lead to the same dangers of success and failure. A matter of life and death was non-negotiable. Her palpable thoughts did not go unnoticed by Sagar.

"Don't fret over the new adventure. You know, after the initial setup, it won't be difficult to get a breakthrough. Funding can't be simpler than this venture," Sagar hypothesized the opportunities.

"Five deaths in accidents are too much of a coincidence! No matter what your conviction, and no matter what the fucking probability calculated by Jim says, I can't pretend there is no grave risk. It is for real, Sagar, and it is baffling to see all three of you turn a blind eye to the threat," Rathishree knew a thing or two about ground reality.

"Now, Rathi, you know I am not backing off after so much preparation into this new venture. Mobile*puri* is for real, and it is going online very soon. We will get a better name for the enterprise. In fact, the inauguration and go-live are not too far away. I am proud of all the background frameworks created by you. You have not only nailed the nature of business with rock-solid PowerPoint presentations, but your engineering scalability is also what will keep us going over the next few months. It is time for you to sit back and see your magic work. I know through the local panipuri vendor Alok that the mafia controlling all those cane mobile sets is for real. Taking into account all the money involved, that threat should be fixed in a jiffy. Now, we should focus more on the work at hand."

She still did not look convinced; he had to try harder. "Yes, startups come with a million problems, and we are here to tame them. With you in my corner, I don't fear anything," Sagar rested the case of the Mobile*puri* venture. The excitement of a startup really cheered up the dismayed girl, and she melted into his arms.

A biker on the prowl sauntered towards VV Puram at 2 a.m. VV Puram has a round-the-clock chain of quick food motels. It is also famously known as Food Street, Khao Galli or Thindi Beedi. A regular eater at the junction, the biker parked the two-wheeler on the central stand. Locking the helmet in securely, the safety gloves stashed in the pouches of the tank-cover, the motorcyclist took a leisurely stroll to the regular stall. Before the biker placed the order, a plate was kept ready for the frequent customer. The dish consisted of three jalebis, a cutlet, four pieces of paddu, two miniature *idlis*, *akki* roti and *ragi* roti. Besides, four quarter-kilo packets of jalebi, *kodubale, kajayam* and *omapodi* along with half-a-dozen *hurana* and *kai holige* parcels were kept ready. The biker visited fortnightly, and the second bill of the month was sponsored by the proprietor. The pleas of the beneficiary were fervently ignored, and it was only after the proprietor threatened to weakly deliver the items at home did the visitor back off from the proposal.

"Why does the panipuri vendor here sell at 50% more price than the usual vendors of other areas?" the biker asked the proprietor.

"We will throw him out of South Bengaluru if he does not increase by 100% by next week. Let the whoreson sell his panipuris elsewhere. No place in Thindi Beedi for that bitchson," the proprietor gritted his teeth in anger.

The owners of the stalls at VV Puram had been on the streets for several decades, and understandably, anybody who set up a new stall needed their blessings.

"Pardon my blasphemy," and the fifty-nine-year-old owner rushed to pick up butter gulkand fruit salad from the Shivanna Gulkand Center, and gave it to the biker.

"Thanks uncle, you take extra trouble to gratify me," the visitor was touched with the impassioned gesture of the stall owner.

The panipuri vendor packed his mobile stall and left. The biker saw the vendor move towards Jain College. After ensuring he had walked two-hundred metres, the key was slotted in the Yamaha RX-100 and the gloves were back on the hands in under five seconds. The second kick put life in the bike engine. The vendor took a right turn on Vani Vilas Road, and the biker followed, pulling ahead by a hundred and fifty metres forward. Stopping the motorbike and killing the engine, the biker drew a mobile out and engaged in a conversation.

The panipuri seller walked fifty metres ahead, and fatigue got the better of him, prompting him to put the mobile shop down. Drawing out the beedi packet, he took three sticks to light up the damn silly smoking pole. Drawing five deep puffs, he felt energized enough to keep going, took the next left and continued walking towards Tagore Circle. When the commuter was down the left street by more than a hundred metres, the biker dragged the bike and carefully observed the next change. Convinced over the straight path of the vendor towards the Nettakallappa Circle, the biker took out the black jacket and folded it firmly over the petrol tank. The bike was put to life on the first kick and taking the longer route through Vidyarthi Bhavan, DVG Road, and zooming at nearly hundred kilometres per hour speed, the motorcycle halted at the Sri Guru Raghavendra Sahakari Bank. The biker was a good two minutes ahead of the vendor and observed him traverse further on the Krishna Rajendran Road. The excellent mint condition of the bike allowed the hawk to turn off all the lights and indicators and silently trail the mobile vendor four hundred metres on KR Road. Satisfied that the panipuri vendor's night home was the ghettos of Wadarabandyapalya near the Yediyur Lake, the biker flew to the bike's garage, a good ten kilometres away.

He was held in the captivity of an eight by fourteen room over the past fifteen months. The deceased entrepreneur's breakthrough, Mohit, was not a one-man show, and he needed capable support provided by Viraj Jain. To celebrate the delivery of the fifty thousand orders over six months, Mohit threw a party for the six mobile vendor boys he was working with. The goal of fifty thousand orders in six months by six boys meant a daily serving of nearly two hundred and fifty orders. The margin of ten rupees per order led to a neat profit of five lakh rupees, and there were twenty times more vendor boys to be conquered and twenty as many cities. The sky was the limit if they could have together seen the next day.

The vendor boys had declined the invitation on completion of every ten thousand successful orders. After four failed attempts, Mohit had given up hope and felt it was futile to even call for celebrations a fifth time. A surprise turned out, and two boys themselves asked for a treat on the completion of fifty thousand orders. The venue was decided a week in advance. While Viraj knew that the risk-taker Mohit had reached out to a host of venture capitalists, the intriguing message of "Big deal coming my way soon. Watch this space for more details", as the Facebook status led to an inquiry, and the simple answer was that he would spill the beans after the party to his parents first and then to him. When they were duly done with the party and came out to pick up their two-wheeler three lanes away, a speeding mini-truck bumped over Mohit. Before Viraj could pick up his friend and partner, a thick metal rod hit his head. When he regained consciousness, the two vendor boys Samir and Jeeva had brought him to this room.

"A personal problem, you see. You and your friend were threatening to take away our business and profits. Fools you take us for, isn't it?" Tiku Singh said, while kicking off their first conversation fifteen months ago.

With his hands and legs tied to the chair and his mouth gagged, Viraj's only option was to nod his head. He cried, begged and shook vociferously, but to no avail. Three days straight, his spirits were broken when he was kept on nothing else but water. The next five weeks were further physical torture when he was treated like a whore in a brothel and given third-degree treatment as a criminal in a cell. The five vendor boys – Samir, Rishabh, Dhyan, Mukesh and Jeeva – verbally cursed him while the physical abuse was always executed by Tiku Singh. Eating and pooping in the same chair ensured his total surrender.

"Software engineer, ha, ha," Tiku laughed at the sorry state of his victim. For the first time, the gag around his mouth was removed. Viraj took that as a sign that he was now allowed to speak too.

"What do you want? Why are you torturing me? I won't go to the police. Trust me," Viraj begged.

"*Chutiye*! Do you think we are scared of the police? A smart engineer like you should know what we expect. You should not make us say it. I hate to say things when you are supposed to already know it, ha, ha," Tiku displayed more cunningness than Viraj's intelligence. He took the cigarette butt and stashed it on Viraj's thigh.

"What do you want? You see, I can't think like a rogue," Viraj winced and admitted his helplessness. How remarkable it is for the torturer that the victim wants to do precisely as per expectations, and now the only remaining task was to complete the specification. Ah! Tiku knew he was an able tormentor, and in his thirty years of experience in the criminal world, he was yet to come across anybody in his captivity who had not broken down.

"You are luckier, you know. We traced your hometown to Ahmadnagar – a place where our network has not yet reached. But we can get it done, and you know what I mean. A message, a call, and a few words... enough to eliminate your family. My boss says they should remain alive, as you should too. Now, look here. You are an engineer, and we want you to trace the next Mohits for us. Refuse, and we will wipe out your family," Tiku was smirking with devil's pleasantry.

"I will help you," Viraj obviously loved his family. He helped the mafia in marking Sripathi and Anjali. When the mafia world was rocked with parallel developments in Pune and Chennai and demanded Viraj to help them with all India insights and leads, he simply shrugged it off saying that he couldn't give all India support. Moreover, each city would require a complete resource. Tiku called his super boss and expressed the problems on the manpower front. The final call was that Viraj should focus on Bengaluru only.

Flat 1304 was left entirely to Rudra and Yashu as Jim and Koyal had respectively gone to their hometowns while Sagar and Rathishree were out on a three-day workshop training sponsored by the company. The fire in the youngest couple's belly towards project Mobile*puri* had long turned cold. Rudra was partly dismayed with his girlfriend because, after the initial impressions, she delivered little on the work front, office included. She was more of a text bookish girl who did not know how to solve technical problems. Besides, she was losing focus by being on her mobile more often than on the laptop.

Rudra could not complain to himself because he had fallen for her beauty and not her brain. Yashu confessed that since cracking the IIT-JEE exams, she simply sleep-walked through the course and allowed her institution's brand label to do the talking for herself.

Yashu was clear about what she wanted. She wanted Rudra to work for her. A few things went wrong with her assessment of Sagar. Though not a bossy kind of person, Sagar expected professionalism from his team and innovation from his flatmates. He was not a fool, and it was after thorough scrutiny that he had zeroed in on Rudra and Jim. Sagar had roped Yashu in their apartment, but the onus of her performance depended entirely on herself first, and Rudra next. While the other four flatmates worked their ass out through the weekend, this duo barely did much, and only Rudra's order-taking from the five helped the matters to soothe out a little of the discomfiture.

Rudra knew it was the right time to be blunt with Yashu and think towards contributing to their future. Sagar might have shown patience all these years, but there was no point in testing him to the extreme. The mentor delivered the results, and now it was for the beneficiaries to back up the faith invested in them. Rudra wanted to be terse with Yashu, and he tried to start it off casually, and then steer towards the more severe issues.

"Sagar's Mobile*puri* efforts benefit us all. I am speechless," Rudra began with a compliment towards the man with a vision.

"Ah, ah! You are quite touchy when it comes to him and Rathi. Tell me, what's your overall growth starting from the four-lakh package?" Yashu asked back. He did not have to repeat it, and his gross package had doubled in two years.

"What about Rathi, Jim and Koyal? Nothing great, isn't it? The foolish girl has taken a forty per cent hit, and now effectively draws a package of mere 3.6 lakhs per annum. Jim has not improved, and his draw is at six lakhs, and Koyal's at four lakhs. Do you know mine? Of course, you do. I draw only a couple of lakhs less than your great Sagar," Yashu knew she could not be counter-argued on the salary front. She was not without her fallacy, though.

A majority of her work in the current office was still done by Rudra himself. He was afraid that if he did not do her share of work, she might hop on to another job. It was not beyond her to try that, and she would do so in a heartbeat. In fact, Rudra already knew what her long calls in the corridor really meant. When Sagar brought her in Flat 1304, he had given her the concession of not paying the rent for the first three months. A full room was dedicated to her, especially the study room. When the lovers were differently aligned, Sagar did not see why he should share her part of the rent. Reluctantly, and without an alternative, Rudra took on the task of paying her ten thousand rupees from his purse.

"You know it is not about the money," Rudra was referring to the excellent platform of Mobile*puri*. "If you take off your rose-tinted glasses, you will see that you were expected to do most of the technological implementation. Scalability is still an issue, and you can showcase your expertise," Rudra wanted her to seriously take up the special role.

"There is always a plan B, my sweety," Yashu knew she could easily flirt her way around Rudra.

"When plan A is all about doing nothing, then plans B to Z are also all about doing nothing," Rudra twitched.

"Do you think I don't know my role, honey," Yashu kissed her boy. Rudra always remained her Plan A in 1304 and their organization. She took off her top and with the last two pieces of undergarments on the body, she could make Rudra dance to her tunes.

For now, Yashu was satisfied with her growth objectives for the year. She did not have to try too hard, and she could simply give the excuse of 'a dumb role' in the current job which did not match her skills and interests, and she would be off to a more satisfactory job in another three to six months. Whenever Rudra wanted to get serious about work, a piece of garment fell off. Yashu believed in the 'friends with benefits' concept. She already freely gave her brand tag to the Mobile*puri* collaboration. Her logic was that if she had to work towards the venture, she must be paid extra to the tune of her salary. Sagar got her perspective quite early during her stay, and by the time he saw that she was not useful, Rudra put his neck out, defending her utility.

"Are you going to work for Mobile*puri* and Accenture forever? Or do you have plans to hitch on different cars?" Yashu asked him as he was inside her.

"Not with the round of funding so close. And then not a second more than the finalization of the early ESOPS for our contribution," Rudra could match her expectations. Growth matters too. Before she could fully comprehend the implication, he smooched her. When the sex is good, the love also grows. Fighting all her senses, the glorious good truth was that Yashu's heart was clearly seduced by Rudra's.

3 The Panipuri Recipe

What's in a name that's not in a brand name? Nothing. Is it true – what name is to a person, is the brand name to a business entity? Beyond the obvious yes, Sagar and Co wanted a snazzy name for their enterprise. An alias that reflected the business, the purpose, the mission, the audience, and where they would be fifty years down the line. A name that achieved all the objectives would most likely project them as a joke. The sobriquet should be dashing though. During the last meeting of the six, it was concluded that the name should be unanimously decided. After all, they were only six thick friends. As a disciplined pack of budding professionals, Koyal shot out the agenda of the next meeting an hour before the scheduled time.

Rudra, as per the assigned role, made the necessary arrangements for the snacks and drinks, and he took care not to disappoint Rathishree. Sagar forewarned him to eliminate needless complications. The five o'clock meeting meant tea/coffee for the beverages, and the three couples planned their independent jaunts to the clubs and pubs after seven in the evening. A lot of chips, samosas, jalebis and Bijnor Chaturvedi Sweets sent by Koyal's parents were displayed splendidly on the dining table. Apart from the snacks, the main agenda as shared by Koyal was the choice of name for the new business entity, the update on the works assigned, the course corrections and realignment of work, if needed.

After two months, the tentative title of Mobile*puri* was marked for shredding. Jim initiated a discussion with the proposal of rejecting the name. "While Mobile*puri* is not really a bad name, I guess we all agree that it can be vastly improved. I just want a more formal confirmation that we agree to shred it," Jim kicked off the debate session.

"Yup, agree. Besides, the name can be mistaken for the breakfast item-puri too," Rathishree concurred. Yashashwini sighed silently over Rathi's acceptance because the tentative title was proposed by the north Karnataka woman, and the idea that it could be improved upon was her lover's.

"Rudra, can you prepare a list of the names we have in our mind. Also, we should try combining words and see how it goes," Sagar proposed. The next five minutes saw the proposals as ePuri, iPuri, APPani, PaaniTech, PPTech, PPuri, NammaPuri, WiPaPuri, etc.

"Oh, by the way, I connected with the host admin of www.pp.com, and they have no objection if we choose PP for our enterprise. However, they want to continue to host their little popular website and won't sacrifice it for our sake. I am not sure how it works out for the cause," Koyal broke an essential piece of news for everyone's contemplation.

"What's the point if we can't host a website with the domain of pp.com and our app is named as PP. It is counterproductive," Yashu pitched in her criticism.

"Yashu, you might be right in thinking in this direction. Obviously, we are not going with PP. But let us not forget that www.pp.com has close to two million subscriptions, highest peak traffic is twelve thousand online users, and most importantly, eight lakhs of its registered users are in Bengaluru. I don't have to say further that most of them are in the age group of fifteen to thirty-five. The admin of the website agreed to one year of free advertisement for our app, and a dedicated blog on their site can be used as per our needs. In the chain email, the admin has argued that the initial popularity of our business can piggy-back ride on their website. It will save us a lot of money, and indispensably get us a lot of customers," Koyal conveyed more details, and added further, "I am sharing the chain email with the admin." She forwarded all the emails for the perusal of the partners.

"I don't endorse using any platform on which we don't have total control. Besides, if the website supports our competitors in future, we will be sitting ducks," Yashu felt she had made valid points.

"Before I go into the details of your communication, Koyal, what is the price for the cooperation?" Sagar was always keen on knowing the cost to the purse strings.

"Oh, that's a pleasant surprise. The admin says that the website is simply for fans of light chaats. He has maintained the website for over eight years, and as such, is satisfied with the revenue generated by the advertisements. Apparently, the owners are fine even without zero revenue and happy to cater to their larger fan base. Effectively, they are charging us nothing," Koyal clarified.

"Is there some catch? Sorry for playing the devil's advocate. Now, we hover over the website and say three months down the line, a competitor replaces us without any warning. We will become laughing stock. Think about it seriously," Yashu was still sceptical.

"Hmm, on the one hand, nobody can deny the undisputed popularity of the website among panipuri lovers. What does the admin say about Yashu's concern?" Sagar wanted more clarity.

"Come on, guys! Somebody is doing charity to you by offering meals, and you are insisting that the sweets must be prepared in pure ghee. Yashu, tell me, how many rivals are there in the offing?" Rudra asked.

"To the best of my knowledge, none," Yashu said simply.

"And you are expecting the admin and owners of the popular chat website to do the R&D for us, and further commit that they will not give their platform to others? What's in it for them?" asked Rudra.

"Rudra, a business deal should be kept in mind with business intent only. We are not taking charity as there is no charity anywhere. So please spare me the humour. Why can't we skip www.pp.com altogether?" asked Yashu.

"Yashashwini has a valid point. And I also understand that the owners are certainly not obliged towards any commitment if they cooperate with us. Can we meet them to discuss more details?" Rathishree enquired.

"Yes, Rathishree, I tried to touch upon this aspect. Turns out that admin, proprietor and owner are one and the same. However, the owner remains anonymous, and unless we hack the website and reveal the owner, we can't even make out the gender of that person. Read all the emails, and you will find how the replies are gender agnostic. So, it is a take-it or leave-it offer. We need to use our own judgment whether to avail the offer or not," Koyal deliberated.

"Ah! I say chuck it," Yashu was clear and sharp.

"Not so fast, Yashashwini. First and foremost, there are no terms and conditions from his end. It means we don't have to choose the name of our enterprise as 'PP' at all. A big plus for us. From our survey and research, it is clear that there is no competitor on the horizon. We advertise ourselves on the damn website, and we will have a strong customer base, something that we badly need to kick off. Let us understand where we stand as of today. We can't afford to pay for a colossal billboarding advertisement. We can't bear the commercial advertisement costs on Facebook or the Google Play Store. Pamphlet expenditure is something that has minimal returns. We plan correctly and make the best use of the www.pp.com offer. Let us now return to the choice of name for our enterprise," Sagar was rational in his assessment. Besides, they couldn't waste the entire discussion hour when other issues were long overdue and needed resolution.

The choices of the names ePuri, iPuri, APPani… went in loops and the consensus deluded the six. When every title was considered four times each, Rudra's suggestion to try a portmanteau of the two words Pani and Puri made more sense than the technicalization of the two words.

"The first two letters of Pani in Pa and last two of Puri in ri combine nicely as 'Pari' which means a fairy. But it is bland," sighed Rathishree.

"What about 'PaPu'?" wondered Jim.

"Oh no, not that infamous name of the six hundred and seventeenth dynastian Rahul Gandhi please," Sagar laughed hard. The laughter continued for five minutes, after which the six got serious again.

"Well, almost there! What do you think about 'PaPi', implying a little harmless sin of ours? With a puri in the closed circles of the three letters P, a and P, and the 'i' marked as a cylinder containing the panipuri water, we should be through with the hunt for the right name," Rudra made the suggestion and drew the idea on a paper.

"It makes sense, I feel," Rathishree approved the plan.

"Amen," Yashashwini endorsed her feelings about Rudra's ideas.

"Koyal and Jim, your take?" asked Sagar.

"A fairly catchy name. That's like 25% work done," Jim gave the go-ahead for the name and Koyal was satisfied with the proposal.

"And that draws my attention to the rest of the 75% work. How is it going, peeps?" enquired Sagar, even as he was most aware of the status, "Yashashwini, where are you on the real-time order synchronization with the GPS marking?"

"Sorry, Mr Bansal, I was overloaded with work at the office. The Accenture project is running behind schedule, and we had one more attrition in the team," Yashashwini passed the buck.

"That's fine. Can you tell me what you will be able to deliver over the next two weeks? Every single day is important towards the launch. What will be your deliverables?" asked Sagar methodically.

"I am trying my level best. So when I get time, I will be on it," promised the newest member.

"That means Yashashwini will be the backup and we need somebody to do the critical real-time synchronization work. No sync will mean disaster implementation of deliveries to the exact customer location," Jim expressed concern.

"I don't have the capability," Koyal regretted she could not be part of the solution.

"Rudra, can you take it up?" asked Sagar.

"No, he can't," Yashashwini finished before her boyfriend could even begin.

"I will try, Sagar," Rudra still tried to overrule his beloved.

"Is it even fair, Rudra? I asked you to lend a helping hand for the same work, and you firmly declined, citing lack of time. After I have failed, I wonder what you mean by trying," Yashashwini scowled.

"Jim, what about you?" Sagar checked.

"Sagar, I am lagging behind even on the current deliverables of the advertisement templates for social media. What I can do is take up the related work to Rathishree's content development. That will release some of her time," Jim tried to create some room.

"Thanks, Jim. I can handover the work to you tomorrow morning, no issues. Now, for the real-time synchronization, I need to first know where we stand from Yashashwini. The website and mobile app development need five working days. This work will require at least seven working days of effort. And these are the optimistic cases bordering on unrealistic targets. Let's hope we will be able to pull through this one. Can you defer your leaving by an hour and hand over the work, Yashashwini?" Rathishree politely asked the flatmate.

"I am afraid there will be no need to defer the departure by an hour as Yashu could not kickstart the work on the real-time synchronization," Rudra cut his girl's uncharacteristic intervention with one of his own.

"Yeah, except for creating the folders, I haven't done anything. Office work was the default priority, you see," Yashashwini showed no regret over her colossal failures.

"Ah! Ok, umm," Rathishree felt no need to express any further.

"But where will you find the time, Rathishree?" asked Sagar.

"Sick leaves and loss of pay! No other recourse," Rathishree had no alternative. In her case, the penalty was very huge as she was already working at sixty per cent salary and work time, and she was not entitled to as many leaves as a regular employee.

Rudra and Yashashwini excused themselves from the meeting and left for their party.

"Completely unreliable and unprofessional. I did not expect this from Rudra. Yashashwini is a serious bane to all the work undertaken until now," Koyal cribbed after the couple had left the building.

"Yeah, even Rudra is delivering only like thirty per cent of the required target," Sagar regretted the collaboration.

"You can see her on the mobile all the time in the apartment. How can she work with such an attitude?" asked Jim.

"Do we really need her brand?" Koyal wondered.

"No, we are not using her brand at all," Sagar clarified.

"I am really wondering how Rathi is tolerating all of this?" Jim put his suspicions into words.

"I am throwing my weight with Sagar. With Jim and Koyal. With the project. There is no time for any of this," Rathishree was clear on what needed to be done.

"Won't it impact your salary, Rathi?" Koyal was concerned.

"Drastically! If it continues in the same way, I will be thrown out in under three months, or even two," Rathishree shrugged at the thought.

"I won't let it happen," Sagar guaranteed and the four high-fived.

"PP RECIPE OF THE MONTH." www.pp.com was not just any fanbase website. Apart from keeping the forum free from spam and junk advertisements, the owner allowed complete democracy. Yeah, there was a reason why any non-chaat discussion was not recognized. However, it was not by the whims of the proprietor, but more because it was the collective decision of its majority of active users. What can be so engaging about a simple website? In the era of smartphones, the users did not miss the website's presence in the app form.

When Koyal reached the admin with a request to advertise their new enterprise, earlier named as Mobile*puri*, the website admin's warmth surprised, and the largesse was encouraging to the six musketeers. Was it a democratic call too? No, every decision in a democracy need not be that of the majority. Besides, the admin reiterated that he was not under any obligation to the users for the simple reason that it was a free platform, not a rights platform. Even then, a user named YBR created a thread with the question, “Should www.pp.com be used freely for new online panipuri sellers?”

“No. The website is for panipuri what Lord’s is for cricket. We should maintain its sanctity,” replied a user named PP101.

“Why not? Online panipuri is just what we all need ,” argued a user RF, a fan of the great Federer.

“Keep pp sane. Don’t dilute it ▲,” another user Nole2011 argued.

“Federer and Djokovic can be friends, but not their fans, ,” PP101 made merry.

“Look PP101, one must love the sport over individuals, no matter how big a star that player might be. Similarly, pp.com is our home, and we must never lose it to filthy advertisements,” fumed Nole2011.

“Stop spamming pp.com,” argued the thread creator YBR.

“Rightly said, YBR,” supported another user named Shivarudra.

The argument and counter-argument went over twenty posts. The admin was not active round the clock, and the debate was getting uglier.

When Jim was checking something on MobileChat, the notification alert of the panipuri website drew his attention. Sagar and Rathishree had left two minutes ago, and Koyal was almost ready.

“Let’s go,” Koyal said, pulling the straps of her sandal.

“Stop, it’s urgent. Call Sagar and Rathishree back. They left just a minute ago and must be in the parking area. Call them back to the flat. It's *urgent,*" Jim was fuming by this time. It was not at all usual for him to lose temper, and Koyal knew something terrible must be brewing. He was stomping up and down the hall when the flatmates returned five minutes later.

"What's the matter, Jim? You look uneasy," Sagar asked.

"Yeah, please look at this thread," Jim showed the burning discussion on pp.com. Sagar read and passed it to Rathishree who later gave it to Koyal. The three could not find anything wrong. The question marks on their faces gave away the fact that they were not getting his concern.

"For god's sake, YBR is Yashashwini B. Rudra, and Shivarudra is our Rudra," Jim had decoded the names of the two users of pp.com. In a shocker, Sagar picked the mobile and reread it with the new information, and he was stunned with the betrayal. Koyal and Rathishree drew their own mobiles and checked, and the pieces fell in place. Jim was now boiling in rage.

"What is her fucking problem?" Koyal was too angry to engage in social etiquettes.

"Jim, there is no doubting that it is Rudra and Yashashwini. Koyal, can you call the admin?" Sagar enquired.

"I am afraid, the admin is really anonymous. The best I can do is drop an email and ask for the thread to be removed," Koyal replied.

"Please do that at once," Jim urged.

"I guess that's not required. The admin has posted, 'Thread locked. pp.com is a free platform and not a rights platform.' But yeah, there is sabotage," Rathishree updated.

"Damn social media. It is too dynamic and devastating," Koyal punched a fist in the air.

"Guys, I know you are all correctly accusing me of favouring Rudra, and rightly so. Even then, please give me some time. I have to marginalize them first and then get rid of it," Sagar proposed a truce.

"Oh shut up, you diplomatic ass! Look, if you don't throw Rudra and Yashashwini out, I won't give a shit to PaPi anymore. Koyal and I walk out right at this instant," Jim was severe.

"I agree. This is nothing less than betrayal. Who's to say… Oh, fuck it all. If you still want Rudra, we are out. Good luck," Koyal supported her boyfriend.

"Wait, guys! This is not just about love and friendship. Trust deficit kills everything. I have to support the right people too, and so I will be with you. Sorry, Sagar," Rathishree too could not take the shit anymore.

"Guys, I am sorry. You are right. I was blinded by stupidity and could not think clearly."

Sagar pulled out his mobile. It took six rings before Rudra received the call with a "Hi!"

Sagar still maintained his temperament. "Return to the flat, immediately." The speakerphone was on.

"What's the matter, Sagar?" Rudra asked.

"Immediately means *immediately*. Over and out," Sagar disconnected.

A message beeped on Sagar's mobile saying that the couple was on their way back. The girl on the pillion seat was not having positive vibes about the night's proceedings.

In a dark closet, a kidnapped engineer switched on the incognito mode of the Chrome browser. Viraj amused himself with ten minutes of porn. Czech beauties always enthralled him, and even in captivity, he could not help browsing for threesome and foursome nudity with one male-only. It bored him after a while, and he then resorted to his favourite game on pp.com. He was creative with his threads, and some of them were very funny.

One sombre day, he created a thread with the title, "*Panipuri ka ling kya hai*?" The Hindi question asked the gender of the golgappa because even non-living entities have gender in this popular language. It became an interesting discussion of its own.

"Definitely female," the famous poster of the forum Liliana added.

"How?" another user Potter asked.

"Both the words paani and puri end with a feminine i. Hence, gender must be definitely female," Liliana laughed.

"By your logic, the complex number *i* must be a female too," Viraj joined the joke.

"Obviously," Liliana added, "It's poetic justice that the complex number, which is also called an imaginary number, is female 😉."

Carrying a little web-search for the meaning of the name, Viraj complimented the user, "I guess apart from meaning the lily flower, innocent, pure, and beautiful, Liliana gets an additional meaning of being imaginary too. I 🖤 you 💐💐💐.."

"The 💐💐💐. are welcome, this is not 💔," laughed Liliana.

"The vanquisher of Voldemort takes his princess Liliana 👩," added Potter.

"I ❤ you, Harry. Blows 💋 on the charming 🤴," Liliana was in love with Potter today.

"Sob, sob, sob, 😟😟😟," Viraj left the discussion.

Taking stock of the time and the expected return of Tiku Singh and others, Viraj knew that he had ample time to converse with somebody online on the web www.pp.com. He was helpless and knew that reaching out to the police was not going to save the day for him. The nexus between his kidnappers and the law enforcing agencies could not be more evident. Two months ago, he got a voice message from his mother, courtesy of out-of-way help from the admin of the website. She had been given his recorded message of four months earlier, and hers was a reply to his. What else could she add beyond the obvious concerns and the relief that he was alive. He could feel helplessness in her voice too. The message to the family as well as himself was clear. Tabs were kept on both ends and smartness from any corner would lead to the termination of the others.

Could he simply keep his fingers crossed and wait for a miracle to happen? He was a goddamn engineer, and he needed to outsmart the ruffians. The two things that he figured out about the admin of the panipuri website were that the server was deliberately located in Russia, and the website owner was definitely an Indian. He was sure that the admin, owner, proprietor, and a few users were undoubtedly one and the same person. The engineer in exile was confident that the user Liliana was a male. It could also be said for sure that the user Liliana must be closely connected with the admin.

The reason was apparent to him, and that was the time zone. Rarely were there any posts from the user when the admin was not around the same time zone. Thus, if nothing more than closer proximity, their residing places must be the same. To a degree, he was tempted to communicate the next set of cryptic messages to Liliana, but then exercised restraint. The admin had been incredible thus far, and he felt it safe to continue texting with him/her.

Message 1: *Liliana must be a man.*

Message 2: *Bosses know about the new online venture.*

Message 3: *Bosses love the roses.*

Message 4: *Few crispy pancakes will be crippled.*

Viraj was aware of the risk he was taking. He was allowed to register on pp.com with the user ID PPwala. Tiku Singh regularly signed in with the same ID. The current user in communication with the admin of the website was PPwila. This was always signed in the incognito mode. Besides, he would delete every received message after reading it. Thus far, he had been able to communicate that the user PPwila and PPwala were one and the same. This was in violation of the forum rules as duplicate profiles were not allowed. Next, he had conveyed the information that he was a kidnapped engineer, and even eight months later, he had not been harmed. It gave him the confidence that he could continue trusting the creator of the panipuri website.

Further, he helped the admin in fixing a bug which provided the site with some safety from hackers. Little did Viraj wager a guess that the virus was a creation of the admin. The kidnapped guy also confided that he had been taken hostage more than a year ago. He spilt the beans over the working of the mafia in the world of panipuri.

Two hours had passed by, and there were no signs of any sound on the trail. The admin had replied to PPwila.

Reply to Message 1: *His balls are still his own.*

Reply to Message 2: *The new bird is as big an idiot as the earlier lot.*

Reply to Message 3: *The butts are for the taking.*

Reply to Message 4: *Be happy, it's not you and me.*

Viraj heaved a sigh of relief, deleted the messages, and closed the incognito browser. He returned to the browsing of porn websites. He smirked at the travesty of his times – browsing porn on the regular browser and useful emails in the incognito mode. At the back of his mind and bottom of his heart, he realized that the website was his only hope to come out of the dark hole he had fallen into.

Rudra and Yashashwini took more than an hour to return to Greenville. Bengaluru traffic is the most unforgiving hellhole in the universe. Parking the bike in the basement, the couple got into the elevator. Rudra was surprised when his girl hit key number 9. When he raised an eyebrow questioning her action, she excused herself that she had an urgent call to make. Yashashwini got out four floors earlier, and Rudra reached the thirteenth floor and rang the bell of flat 1304.

"Where is Yashashwini?" asked Sagar. He was clearly in a foul mood, and Rudra had never seen him in such furore in the five years of acquaintance.

"What's the matter, Sagar? I am sorry, but the party seems to be ruined. I don't get the problem," Rudra politely replied.

"Get her first," Sagar insisted. He was clear that the other three will not be a part of the fury. After all, the buck stops at him, and he had picked up the mantle decisively.

"You know she takes hours on calls," Rudra said. He had a hunch that the 'matter' was something related to her, and he had to shield her at all costs. "Tell me, Sagar, what's the problem," Rudra had a feeling that things were likely to get ugly.

"If he wants it this way, so be…" Jim was not allowed to complete his opinion.

"Jim, stop! Please, trust me to do the right thing. I am not Dhritharashtra to be blind to that degree as you are taking me to be. Rudra, I don't care where she is, or how long she usually takes on her calls. Go out and get her. *Now!*" Sagar was clear.

"Fine! I'll be back," Rudra assured and went down the stairs as she was indeed on another call when he called her up. Two minutes and three floors down, he saw her busy on a call. She put her call on hold and looked at him.

"What's the matter?" she asked Rudra.

"The team wants you. *Now*," Rudra wanted her to join immediately.

"Rudra! I don't care for this PaPi and the team. Please. First, you spoiled the night, and I am starving. Now you won't even allow me to speak with my cousin. Look, tell the team to *fuck off*," Yashu was furious.

Rudra decided he was not going to be caught between his girl and the team all night long. Besides, he did not understand why they were so angry with her. It had to end, and he was the go-between. As much as he loved Yashu, there was a limit to his tolerance. The team had already suffered hell because of the two of them. Even now, he was clueless about the core issue, and there was only one way to figure it out. Yashu had already returned to her cousin's call and ignored him.

"*Mala thau nahi kay, lach lach la…*," Yashu was cribbing to her cousin in Marathi that she was not aware of the nuisance created by the so-called team and she was fed up with them. A shocker came her way when the mobile was snatched out of her hands, and Rudra disconnected the call. Glaring furiously at her, he grabbed her wrist and dragged her upstairs. When they were on the landing of the tenth floor, she was in agony and begged him to release her wrist and agreed to cooperate with him and talk to the team. Rudra conceded the request, and two minutes later, the couple was in their apartment. Rudra now begged Sagar to come clear on the problem.

"She knows it already. Here!" Sagar handed over the laptop which had a tab opened in the browser. The website was, of course, pp.com and the thread opened was "Should www.pp.com be used freely for new online panipuri sellers?"

Rudra's face turned blue on reading the discussion. Of course, YBR was Yashu's account on the website, and he was Shivarudra. He did not make those posts on the thread, and the timings clearly reflected the ugly truth. His mobile was with Yashu, and he was driving at that time a few hours earlier. Yashu had not only created the thread, but also replied on the same using his account. She had clearly betrayed the team, and this backstabbing was the last thing he could expect.

He felt as though he had been slapped!

"I am sorry, really, really sorry. You don't deserve this, none of you. I, I..." Rudra's eyes moistened. He couldn't have thought of betraying Sagar, and this betrayal knocked the wind out of his sails.

"Rudra, I just want to add one thing. Yashashwini is mistaken in her thinking that we are cashing in on her brand name. I have always been aware that she's done almost nothing since cracking her entrance exam five years ago. What was required was her sharpness and engineering acumen, and what we got is there for you to see. You both are now *out*," Sagar delivered the verdict that they were not welcome anymore.

"Ten minutes to pack your bags," Rudra told Yashu and stormed into their bedroom and began packing his belongings. Two minutes later, he came out with a trolley bag and addressed Sagar, "I am really sorry for this, Sagar. I feel humiliated. For other things, I will come after a week or two. Sorry, team, and I mean it." He was aghast and despondent. He warned Yashu to get packing.

Yashashwini had not realized the quantum of her actions. She had never once felt that the team would go for such a drastic action when she created the contentious thread. Her impression was that she was an indispensable part of the team. Her belief all along was that her IIT brand label was a necessity for the group. Sagar's disclaimer hit her harder than he might have intended.

"T...te... team," Yashu now stuttered in disbelief, "Can I please get one night here to… to gather myself… pl… please. Sagar, please."

He nodded.

The ramshackle room cum house was filled with the smell of gutkha. The pungent onion smell and rotting sewer below was the hallmark of the lives of the poor vendor men. In the ruins and gutter, Barfi could still smell the sweet rose. It had been over two months since Shikhan had been sacrificed to satisfy to the bloodthirst of their boss Jaani. The substitute would generally arrive in two weeks, and yet there were some hindrances this time around. However, none of the five occupants – Alok, Barfi, Jarokh, Bholu and Ghumroo – complained. The luxury of moving their asses while sleeping without touching another body would end any time, and they had to enjoy it while it lasted. Barfi had to double up Shikhan's region too, and it meant he had to start much earlier than his filthy peers.

"*Kya be harami Barfi... kaisi kat rahi hai teri jhand zindagi?*" Bholu laughed at Barfi's plight. Barfi had to first go to National College and begin his mobile shop at 10 a.m. A month earlier, he had cribbed to Jaani that the sales were almost zero in the early morning time and nobody purchased much until three in the afternoon. After 2 p.m., he was to move the unit to Vijaya College. The reward for the cribbing was a slap on the face and two hard punches in the belly.

As there is a mirage in the desert, Barfi found his own happiness in this hell. The purpose of sending Barfi early in the morning to the National College was barely sales and profit. Even when there are lesser animals to hunt in the jungle, the big cats need to periodically leave their scent to mark the territory. Barfi realized that he was Jaani's piss and had to remain posted at National College until the replacement arrived.

Desperate times create more opportunities, and the early morning walk to the college opened a different avenue for Barfi. Jaani and the higher-ups were aware that there would be zero sales until three in the afternoon, and hence this time would be a vigil free time. The sixth day when he was walking towards the college, a woman in her mid-twenties stopped him at the seventh cross street. The voice came from a temporary shed of an almost deserted corner site.

"*Idhar bhaiya, idhar*," she drew his attention. "*Bihar se ho?*" He nodded to her enquiry. The lady was from Bihar too, working as a cheap labourer.

"I am Barfi. What's your name?"

"Kamali. I have been living on boiled water for the past three days. Give me some panipuri. It will be a great favour," the woman almost begged.

Eating panipuri for breakfast is a bad proposition. This woman had not eaten for three days, and he knew consuming the tamarind-spiced water with *puri* prepared in adulterated oil would be a disaster for her.

"Come with me," he asked her to join him. "Where do you live in Bihar?"

"Sasaram, Rohtas. And you?" Kamali asked.

"Manihari, Katihar. We are far off in Bihar, and so near over here, isn't it?" he moved on, carrying his mobile unit.

Three streets down the line, he stopped at a pushcart selling idlis and dosas. He asked the small hotelier to give the lady five idlis, and he helped himself to four idlis and a vada. Two teacups and twenty minutes later, he paid for both of them, and also slipped twenty rupees into her hand.

For the next two weeks, Kamali and Barfi dug more into one another. She was six years older than him. Four days before her approaching him, she had lost her job and was recouping from fever. Her husband had moved her to the shed eight months ago and had deserted her on the second day of the relocation. When Barfi asked her if she suspected another woman in her husband's life, she clarified that she was the other woman and laughed. He hinted that he wanted to speak about important issues with her. He could not park the mobile bamboo unit and step inside for an hour. The problem was he could not leave an hour earlier, which would definitely lead to suspicion. On the way home the previous night, he asked her to be awake at 5 a.m.

Setting the alarm at 4.30, and using the alarm tone the same as his ringtone, he woke up at the scheduled time pretending to receive an incoming call. He blasted the usual hello-hello trick and cursed the caller of the wrong number so early in the morning. Then pretending that he had lost sleep, he skipped out of the room for an early morning walk.

Walking to the corner site, he knocked on the door and sneaked into the shed. Hesitatingly, he asked Kamali if she anticipated her husband's return.

"I think these hands will then become the hands of a murderer," Kamali was clear that she did not want to have anything more to do with the man who had deserted her. He asked her if she thought of returning to her home town in Rohtas. She declined saying she had got a maid's work in three more households, and that would see her through the day. She promised to return all the money he had spent on her over the past two weeks.

"I will not take money from you, Kamali," he said it in his own romantic style.

"Why will you not take the money from me, Barfi?"

"I will take you, not your money," and saying so, he hugged her tightly and kissed her madly. She too yearned for him. Over time, the two had decided to become one.

The morning in flat 1304, Greenville, was the same as it was every other day, except for the couple that let down the team. Jim and Koyal resumed their ritual work at 6 a.m., and Rathishree had awakened at 5 to kick start the work on real-time data synchronization. Sagar, well, he had a million pieces to close, and he was working until 2 in the morning. He would not wake up until 7 a.m. The room that wore the look of mourning was of Yashashwini. She tried to bridge the difference between herself and Rudra. However, he could melt her down with his fury, such was his anger. She did not get sleep until 3 in the morning.

At 7, when she had woken up, she saw that Rudra had packed all of his belongings. "Bloody pack your bags," he warned her as she was getting up. Yashashwini had different ideas. When she heard the clattering sounds from the kitchen, she got up knowing who would be there at the stove.

Rathishree was shocked to see that her rival was up so early. Taking it as the last of the surprises, she continued her work and focused on preparing some excellent decoction. She could make out that Yashashwini was standing still and intending to say something. However, it was not her problem, and she did not appear as somebody who thrives on others' miseries.

Yashashwini first cleared her throat and drew the attention of her bete noire, "Rathishree, I just wanted to clarify that I am really sorry for my pathetic behaviour towards you. I have been a real bitch. If possible, please forgive me. I am fine if you don't want to say a word to me." Yashashwini decided to wait for a good minute because she had a lot of apologies to offer. She felt the first and foremost person she should be apologizing to must be Rathishree.

"Your inefficiency was a different story. It is not for me to forgive you because it is normal to find people like you in a team and an organization. With what you did yesterday, you let down Sagar, and he is the one who can decide on your apology," Rathishree clarified.

"Sorry, Rathishree! I regret being salty and bitchy towards you most of the time. Yesterday's offence is unforgivable, but can you forgive me for the day-to-day bickering in the past?"

"Would you even care? Especially if you had not been caught outright yesterday?"

"I wouldn't have, if not for yesterday's blowout. However, of all the stupidity that I have done over the past six months, I am convinced mistreating you is the severest for which I must be reprimanded," Yashashwini's voice now carried sincerity. Yashashwini's arrival in the kitchen had caught Koyal's attention, who now entered the kitchen too.

"It does not matter," Rathishree did not know what to make of the apology and shrugged off the offering, "Hi, Koyal! Just two minutes, the coffee will be ready." She hesitated for a second and then continued, "What about you, Yashashwini? Coffee?"

"Sure," she was now ready to grab on to whatever would be thrown her way. It would help to get as much time with anybody over remaining in isolation.

"Fine, team. Coffee in five minutes," Rathishree screamed.

An awkward silence graced the dining table with the elephant in the room. Rudra was there to ensure that his girlfriend did not cause any more embarrassments. Sagar kept silent because he did not wish to speak with the two. Jim and Koyal were out of words, and Rathishree only used one word 'coffee' while handing over one cup to each of them. Sagar was sipping faster than usual as he wanted to clearly see the back of the two at the earliest.

"Sagar, I am really sorry for my action. In my single-minded madness to prove that I am better than Rathishree, I played dirty. In fact, the blindness was to the degree that I didn't even realize I was destroying the team. I have asked her forgiveness, and I now ask each of you. Sorry Jim, sorry Koyal, and sorry Rudra," Yashashwini said at the cost of appearing silly and repetitive.

Sagar kept his silence, and nobody else bothered to clear any further air. Even Rudra half-opened his mouth and then shut it again. When his cup became empty, Sagar got up and felt that as the team leader, he needed to end the mess.

"Rudra and Yashashwini, you might both consider staying one more day and drag your asses out tomorrow," Sagar shot the message and left for his work.

Rudra could not miss his mentor's hidden message, and he was sure something significant was bound to happen by the end of the day. The other three too realized the same, and it was just that they could not be bothered anymore.

Independent of the contribution to PaPi, the office work was an entirely different ballgame. Yashashwini was fired from her job by 11 a.m. Her lackadaisical attitude did not go unobserved by the HR, and there were more than half-a-dozen complaints against her being on the mobile all the time at her desk. She was anyway under a probation period of six months. Rudra could cover for her lack of contribution, but not for lack of attitude. The HR was completely blunt in their feedback and demolished her ego to smithers.

The humbled Yashashwini returned to the flat and sought thirty minutes of Sagar's time. She was now under no misconceptions regarding her capabilities and begged Sagar for a shot at redemption. The unemployed lady argued that more hands were certainly required at PaPi, and if not for any other reason, she would like to contribute in a way to clear her share of the rent for the past six months. Her offer was that she would undoubtedly move out to a PG hostel, but contribute to the real-time data synchronization problems.

Sagar did not take a decision by himself. He summoned a quick fifteen-minutes meeting with the four of them, and then the collective call was to allow Yashashwini and Rudra to stay back and monitor their work ethic.

There was no looking back, and this panipuri had undergone all the hassles to hammer out a delicious dish.

Sagar and Rathishree burned the midnight oil along with peanuts, tea, coffee, chips, doughnuts and a lot of carbonated drinks to wash it down. During the last visit, Sagar's mother had rightly pointed out that he was overworked and needed to catch a break. The flatmates extended the idea to Rathishree too. Little did anybody anticipate, Rathi included, that Sagar would take his girl along to Phuket. Bansals were more conservative, and Rathi's folks were beyond orthodox. Only Jim's parents were accommodative of the live-in status, and primarily because the duo promised marriage soon. The star-crossed holidaying lovers put a cover on their little affair from their parents. They might not ever need to reveal it either.

When Sagar discussed the Phuket holiday, Rathishree thought it was his wishful thinking. When he asked for her passport, she felt it was indeed a possibility. She was totally in the holiday mood after he flashed the tickets. She hugged him the tightest and his eyes might have dropped to the floor if she had not broken the hug and kissed him on the mouth in the common hall. It was the first time she had expressed herself so blatantly, shocking all her flatmates. The impulse was spontaneous, and only she was capable of it in the false-coloured world, according to Sagar. He was happy and only wished for her to be more forthcoming.

The full mode on Rathishree proved to be a bag of energy that contained a million suns.

4 The New Dawn

Rathishree was totally in the holiday mood. The stress of working incessantly over the last six months had taken a toll on the brilliant engineer. The fun break was just what they needed.

When the beer was served on the flight to Phuket, Sagar realized that he did not know much about Rathishree's personal life, except that her family hailed from north Karnataka. She started off her career with Rudra in the same company, and the duo fell in love in the first couple of months itself. Sagar felt it was the right time to know about each other.

"Rathi! Why do you get irritated when Rudra calls you by your short name?" Sagar took a sip of the beer and looked into her eyes.

"Ah! Obvious, isn't it? Can you board a flight with a cancelled ticket? He wants to eat the cake, digest it, and then have it too. I don't doubt his meanness, and almost guarantee it, knowing him for close to two years. He is a buffoon, and it was not a coincidence and more of an enactment by him and Yashu when we found them in the park. The drama as if he was caught offguard is the stuff made of dumb Bollywood movies.

Predictable as shit!" Rathi could see through the conspiracy, and she was sure Sagar understood it well too.

"I thought the same too. The only reason I have overlooked it is our coming together. It looks selfish. If somebody did to me what Rudra did to you, I would have thrown that person out of the flat long back. Yet, the selfish me overlooked Rudra's overt ways and ignored his betrayal to you. Sometimes, I get very angry with myself," he was disappointed with himself.

"That's fine, love. Probably the same reason why I overlooked their apathy. I would have moved out of the flat if Cupid had not bound us," she took her lips to his, and the two had a five-second smooch under the dimmed lights of the plane.

"What about your family? I don't know too much about them and apologies for asking now," Sagar said, almost blushing.

When Rathishree was first introduced by Rudra to Sagar and Jim at the time of her moving in, the firm and confident young girl was definitely a force to reckon with. Her positive energy and vibes would easily rub on to everyone around her, and she turned out to be a pure vegetarian who was also a beer and gin lover.

Jim had once hypothesized that her family must be as forthcoming as herself, and that had prompted both Rudra and Rathi to spill the beer they were sipping. Rathi's family was a devout Lingayat family who would have roasted her alive on finding out that she drank alcohol, even if she was a social and party drinker. Her father Tukaram Kannur was a six-time MLA from the Kalaghatgi taluk of Hubli district. With strong saffron representation from the area, her father benefited from the ancestral roots in the Sangh. A two-time minister in the fractional tenure of the saffron party meant the girl did not have to really bother about academic stuff at all. The intercaste marriage of her parents inculcated the inclusive nature in her. Her mother Mahamanasi was a school teacher who did not give up teaching even when she married into the affluent family. The strong sense of integrity and academics imbibed by her mother meant that Rathi remained grounded and compassionate. While her two elder brothers were not much different from the girl, everybody cannot resist power and affluence. Regular visits to her mother's family made a difference in Rathi's outlook towards life. Among the eight siblings, her mother was sixth in line. This teacher from the scheduled backward caste community toiled a lot for the betterment of the poor. Though the teacher was undoubtedly helped by the financial might of her husband's political influence, she was proud of her ability as an academician and not embarrassed for not harnessing dreams of higher degrees.

"My goodness, so you are the daughter of the PWD Minister! I can't believe it. Did Rudra know?" Sagar suspected.

"Yes, and that was one of the reasons why he was disappointed with me. My outright refusal to use influence in any manner. I hate to be given anything on a platter," Rathi asserted.

It all made sense as the loop completed itself. Rathi earned her place in their apartment first. She slogged her way through the projects and made the necessary sacrifices. Apart from the significant role in setting up the platform for the app development, Rathi would do the survey, research and market insights on the investors' moods. She had correctly stopped Sagar and Rudra from pitching the proposal three weeks ahead of the right time. None of the credit was simply bestowed based on a mere partner or her dangerous sex appeal.

"Whatever my limited knowledge about this region, my guess is that your maternal side of the family must be non-vegetarian. When you go to your maternal grandparents' home, how do you resist the tempting non-veg?" asked Sagar.

"It wasn't too difficult for me to resist non-veg food. I was born nine years after my parents' marriage, and mom had long turned into a vegetarian. She wasn't too fond of non-veg food to begin with, she told us. And whenever we visited my grandparents' home, the focus was more on providing sweet savouries over non-veg. I have no issues having my food with non-vegetarians around me. What about you? I guess we did not get time to discuss your family?" Rathi asked him.

"Ah! Same as your paternal side of the family, I will be roasted if caught eating non-veg. Eggs and mushrooms are the limits for me. On the power front, no. My parents and grandparents are not powerful, politically speaking. However, it is not too difficult to reach out to the influential among distant relatives, if required. But it is terrific to dig in our heels and get a couple of VCs on board. Seriously, though, without your taking a hit in the salary pay and working four days in a week, we would not have reached the PaPi stage this sooner," Sagar gave her due credit.

Sagar's contact with the other Bansal made networking easier for the venture. Socializing with the biggies of Greenville provided the right connection in the world of VC funding. However, there was work to be done, and nothing was going to be smooth. Rudra's silence had many reasons, and failure on the contribution front was at the very top. After the initial enthusiasm tapered off, Rathi was the first one to cross the goal post. She did not jump on her ex-lover's part of the work, and instead assisted Sagar with other errands.

The much-awaited engagement date was finally zeroed in on by Koyal's parents – a fortnight after the inauguration of PaPi.

"Congratulations, hon! I love you," said Koyal after announcing the engagement date agreed by all the involved parties. The initial discussion included the personal matters, the dress for the occasion, the friends and relatives to be invited and the agony aunt rambles too. Two hours after grinding out all personal matters, the topic reverted towards the behaviour of the youngest couple of their flat in Bengaluru.

"It is good that Yashashwini is mending her ways," Koyal mentioned.

"Ha, ha," Jim laughed, countering the belle's belief.

"Oh, you are still suspecting?" Koyal had clearly missed observing a few things.

"I will not blame it on your naivety. Sagar has clearly erred in pardoning her and Rudra. Her getting fired was unexpected, and beyond giving her a long rope, there are little benefits. Rathi does not want to prove her lover wrong and hence the leeway. Anyway, only time will tell us how long Yashu's dedication will last," Jim was rational enough.

Sagar and Rathi enjoyed two days of great vacation. The booze and sex in the night did not count as a Phuket speciality, and hence, almost guiltily, they indulged in six hours stay at the Kata Noi beach and the Nai Harn beach. Rathi went beyond the beer and gin while enjoying the rum at The Chalong Bay Rum Distillery. Sagar might have been her mentor back at home, but he was her boyfriend in Thailand, and hence it was his statutory duty to do the shopping for her as per her fancy at the night market.

By the afternoon of the second day, when the taxi was about to take the couple to the Buddha statue, the duo simultaneously asked the driver to direct the steering towards the Perfect Phuket Mai Khao Resort. If the driver had delayed reaching the resort by five minutes, the couple would have commenced making love in the car itself. The driver could vouch that the couple was aware of no public kissing in Thailand, and that was the only reason for their restraint. He anticipated that the couple would pay him by cash and forfeit the change, and he was not wrong.

Sagar picked up a whiskey and gin along the way to their little castle. As soon as the door shut behind them, he picked her up and locked his lips with hers. Rathi wrapped her legs around his waist, and his hands squeezed her hips remorselessly. It would be a decidedly wild session in the offing, and she was waiting for it for a while. She declined the gin and picked up whiskey, corking it open.

RaSa as one possible portmanteau of their names translated from Hindi to English means the pleasure of life. SaRa as another portmanteau might indicate completion. The combination RaSa and SaRa as RasaSara implies the closure of the loop known as the joy of life, which is what the two were trying to accomplish in the Phuket resort.

Moving his lips down her chin, neck and bosom, he gripped the first button of her trendy parrot green shirt tightly between his lips. She liked the prospect of his unbuttoning each of the ten with his mouth and not his hand. She was clearly in for a surprise. The first-time worn shirt was elegant, but not torn free.

Too many things were happening at the same time, give and take a second here and two seconds there. Rathi's regret was not that the new shirt was torn. She did not anticipate the rash move from the artistic Sagar she knew him to be. It was akin to a werewolf ripping the skin out of the prey. Why was she then feeling more loved than being fearful? The swift astonishment was the effortless manner in which he pulled it off.

The torn shirt was lying on the ground, her left bra strap was slid down, and the mound was in his mouth. She was moaning as he bit her nipples and his hands took the bra out of the equation.

She wanted to ask a million questions. How did he have this enormous raw power? Why did he assume she would be okay with his wild ways? On her especially? Why was she moaning when she should be truly angry with him? When did questions on his actions turn into problems on her reaction? Besides, she asked herself now, if her intent was a protest, why was she unbuckling his belt? Holy crow, if not cow, when did he get rid of her short pants and leave her in her panties?

He raised his hands in the expectation that she would take off his upper garments. She did not disappoint him. She stood up and picked up the whiskey as the lovely pair entered the bathroom. All of the earlier proximity was either in darkness or in dim light. It was the first time the two unabashedly went madly at each other in the daylight. A concurrent giggle at the thought and he again roughly fondled her, pressing her breast against his bare chest. She winked at him and indicated that he should carry her to the bathtub.

"I swear it will be like the first time," he promised Rathi as he slid into the tub first, and then gently pulled her, and she slipped in as a fish finds its way in the water. Two layers of love! As she entered the tub by immersing the foot first, in sync with his pulls and slips, it was a sensual experience.

"Do you know why sex in water is always exhilarating?" Sagar asked her while moving his hands all over her back.

"No," she did not want to venture any guess, and neither did he ask the question to find an answer. Any attempt of hers to provide it would be a damper.

"Water is life, and hence you, me, and water make for a threesome," he slid down his head and brought hers too fully under the water. The underwater kiss was more prophetic because his legs were now in the air and she was flapping hers after fifteen seconds in action. Using his ankles deftly, Sagar artistically pulled their heads out of the water without breaking the kiss. The see-saw between the head and foot continued until the kiss was eight minutes old.

"Air is also life, isn't it? Why is it then not as romantic when the water is absent?" Rathi asked a valid question.

"Ah, you are a damn lusty hottie who wants a foursome," he winked and flipped over and surprised her with a few quick entries as fast as the bubbles created by the strokes in the water.

The first time they had met, love was certainly not a possibility between them as Rathi was Rudra's girl. When Sagar had conducted her interview over nearly two hours, he was convinced that she was a lady who lives up to her words, and beyond the implied and understated assurance. He did not take Rudra's words at face value and insisted that he needed to check her compatibility with the rebellious goals of flat 1304 residents.

Sagar had dated two women earlier. The first girl Vaidehi Swarup was his consistent love from high school until the early graduate years. When he went to BITS Pilani, she stayed back at Vidisha, and the distance killed the relationship after she found a better guy too soon. The second woman Ananya Sengupta was an early date in Bengaluru and at the close of his probation. Both of them were freshers, and she found his overt interest in her job confirmation from trial to regular employment a bit too much. As he tried to help her jump over the tide towards the approval, she opted on joining another company. He focused on making a mark in his career over another love interest.

Barfi found it extremely difficult to resist Kamali. The early morning erroneous calls became a norm. He would get up to the self-set alarm, pretend that the signal was weak, and walk out of the shanty. Even as he was doing this out-of-context behaviour on the average of three times a week, he was lucky that none of his roommates turned on him. A little of his nirvana also lay in the delay of Shikhan's substitute. Jaani's body language revealed no hurry in the recruitment of the new boy. The economy was improving everywhere, and impoverished families were difficult to find. Besides, there was intense competition between Jaani's spread over the country, and the supplying states were much lesser, not more than four.

Kamali also warmed up nicely to him. Doubtless to say that after she found work at three households, her earning was pretty decent. She did not repeat it, but it was clear that her husband was done for good. The owner of the small shed where she lived was also the occupant of the adjacent lavish bungalow. As long as she did the mopping and cleaning work four times in a week, they did not bother what the maid did in her hut.

A beautiful morning, he barged into her home as usual and leaned against the compound wall. The tea was boiling, and she added crushed ginger for extra flavour and distinct taste. "*Tere liye kadak chai*," she boasted of having made special tea for him.

"*Terese zyada kya kadak hogi*," he complimented that the tea couldn't be more special than her. He realized that he could not buy her anything so early in the morning, or even take something safely to the room at night. There were two primary reasons for this. First, the risk of Jaani finding out, which would mean the end of him. The second reason being no hiding and/or private place in the room. Everything belonged to everybody. He could not even drop the purchases in her compound while walking back around midnight because the chances of getting caught by either Jaani or his roommates was enormous.

"Who all are there in Manihari?" asked Kamali.

"Only my father must be alive. Mai was too sick, and she's not likely to have made it so far," Barfi told her, sipping tea from the porcelain mug. He knew that she was independent. He was not.

"Hmm," she drew tea from her mug. Already attracted to his side, she rubbed her soft cheeks against him. She thought many times during the day if she was being fair in seducing him. Not only was he six years younger than her, there was nothing but risk for him. Unlike her, he had a family to support in his hometown. All that thinking was just a wasted exercise because she was madly in love with him. Apart from the help during her troubled days, he literally took excellent care of her. Lending her money at regular intervals, using a condom every time he entered her, etc., conveyed to her that she could not find a better lover than him.

The door flung open, and the Bihari couple felt tremors. Their hearts were in their mouths, and they spilt the hot tea on themselves. The person who barged in threw a black polythene cover stuffed with some bundles. The head was covered in a full-face helmet, and the biker threatened the lovers, "An autorickshaw is waiting for you two streets down the line. Sit in it and go wherever the driver takes you. Any deviation from the instructions and that will be your last thought." The biker was holding a large butcher's knife and warned to use it if the orders were not followed.

"But we have nothing to…" Kamali tried to speak up.

"Shut up!" said the machinated voice and swung the knife frighteningly in the air.

Without any alternative, Kamali and Barfi followed the instructions. The bike was RX-100, and the duo found an auto-rickshaw waiting for them.

The lull in the online activity over panipuri beginnings worried Tiku Singh. He tormented the captive engineer, but was not able to gain any new insights. The Stockholm syndrome had long set in, and Viraj retorted with his own twists, in words at least. Today marked a different story, and the three masked big shots came together for the half-yearly review at Singh's den.

The underworld peers Jaani and Tiku had updates with the session chaired by their undisputed boss Baja. The three always wore scarves across their faces, and none of the Aloks, Barfis, Dhyans, Jeevas or the Virajs would be able to identify them in the street. Tiku's worries over a lack of insight were essentially Baja's.

"Munda kaam ka hai kehat ho. Chhe mahinon se sirf paani ke patashe khaye jaa raha hai, aur mutate. Kuch nikla naa, iski gand mein aise ghusedunga ki muh se bahar nikalega randi ke," Baja said in chaste Hindi. Abused, more than stated. He cribbed over the zero insights during the past six months, even after restricting the search zone to the Silk City only. In the eventuality of something escaping the engineer's intelligence, the main head guaranteed to get ugly.

"Bigado naa, mere sarkar. Ye to hamara Theon Greyjoy hai, Reek," Tiku smirked and ruffled his hand in Viraj's hair. In the fourth month of kidnapping, the first concession granted was the use of the Internet for personal entertainment. When Viraj was browsing for some clippings of *Game of Thrones* on YouTube, the fascinating snippet of the Trial by Combat between Bronn and Ser Vadis at Eyrie fired Tiku's imagination. The fall of Ser Vadis through the moon door brought the devil's heart in the mouth, and that kicked off the fascination of the *Game of Thrones* to the

kidnapper, later his peer Jaani, and little more than to their little godfather Baja. The magnificent fantasy world of GRR Martin became their entertainment point, and they would ask Viraj for clarifications whenever they were not able to follow some story arc. It went without saying further that Theon's defiling as Reek by Ramsay Snow was their favourite part.

"*Kaunse Ambani ya Adani aanewale hai ye paani ke patashe mein bamb phodne*," Viraj belittled the business of panipuri. He mocked the kidnappers by chiding that the profits of the entire business combined were not going to attract the attention of the real business magnets. That made his search that much more difficult because the hunt among the millions was going to nought multiple times. "*Pakda to hai billi ko is pinjare mein, noch lo*," he then revealed that a new kid was in there on the block, trying to make a bit of fortune again through the online sales of panipuri.

Koyal Mehra's post on www.pp.com detailed the new venture intently branded as PaPi. The thread on the panipuri forum talked about a new initiative in the making by three young entrepreneurs – Sagar Bansal, Rudra and Jim. The initial service zone of the new business was to be HSR Layout. The coverage would then slowly extend to Belandur, EcoSpace, Embassy Tech Village and Marathahalli.

"Who are the boys over there?" Baja asked from under his scarf.

"Fifty-two of them," Jaani could crunch the numbers as fast as a computer when it came to his jurisdiction, "Pakya, Dhiraj, Sailesh, Jarokh, Sriram…"

"*Abbe gandu,*" Baja was furious over the comprehensive database when he wanted the precise answers, "I want the boys in HSR Layout."

"Oh, only around HSR? I have four boys – Alok, Jarokh, Bholu and Ghumroo. What can they possibly know about the new online PaPi?" Jaani wondered.

"*Bhosdike, sab kuch ye chhokra karega?* I expect your boys to figure out details too," Baja said furiously. He was aghast that their network of so many boys on the field was practically useless to prevent the online sales assault.

"I am tired of asking the IT SEZ areas for myself. I promised twice the income and ten times the insights. But you will listen only to the old Jaani," Tiku cribbed.

"*Tu phirse chalu ho gaya,*" Jaani yelled at his subordinate. He was furious that Tiku felt it was the ripe time to swap the areas allocated to them by the notorious Baja, "Don't forget, you were soiling your underwear when I was ruling this pensioner's paradise."

"Tell me whether it is his boys who have got the lead over the PaPi or my Reek," Tiku loved to drive his point that he was the saviour once again.

Tiku Singh long aspired to take over the chunk of IT zones allocated to Jaani. The competition is fiercest in the crime world. In the relatively less notorious panipuri sales too, the smaller vendors were managed by the likes of Jaani and Tiku, and they were in turn controlled by Baja. Among the three of them, Jaani was the first arrival in the city with a team of fourteen boys to capture the then available market for the golgappa's cheapest mode of sales. Eight of the first batch were moved to other cities, and the remaining six were dumped in the gutter. Jaani was never a pushover and only after a bloody battle which involved more casualties for Baja, it was possible to assert his authority. It was almost a dummy advantage and pushed too hard, Jaani would take it to blood over a compromise. Besides, handing over the region to Tiku, even if the newest powerhouse promised more exploitation of salespoint, meant Jaani was losing his mojo and such a snub would have violent repercussions. What was getting uglier was the discussion happening in the presence of their Reek.

"I will think about your demand if this bastard helps five more times," and Baja punched Viraj hard in the stomach, forcing the engineer to collapse on his knees and throw up two minutes later.

A gentleman accompanied by a lady strolled along the Sajjan Rao Road, VV Puram, adjacent to the famous Food Street. The idea was to buy a used automatic scooter at a much-reduced price. The rise in raw material costs and higher emission compliances had sky-rocketed the prices of two-wheelers.

The lady's choice was none other than Vespa Elegante 125. The gentleman promised to take her to the street of used two-wheelers, and list all the models of the Vespa brand, and then choose one model.

Twenty-four of Vespa's Elegante 125 and 149, SXL 125 and 149, and VXL 125 were on sale in the street. The models varied from six months to six years, one to three ownerships, and the odometer reading ranged from four thousand to sixty thousand. However, nothing fluctuated as much as the price, and the cheapest was available at thirty-five thousand, and the most expensive was only ten thousand short of the on-road price.

During the conversation with different shop-keepers, the gentleman spoke in Hindi and English to help his girlfriend follow the dialogues. When the choice was narrowed down to four scooters, he broke into the native language to extract maximum mileage in the bargain. Of the four models selected by the girl, the least priced used two-wheeler was fifty-five thousand rupees, and the guy proved out to be one heck of a bargainer. He impressed his girlfriend by getting the scooter at a mere forty-two thousand rupees, and a helmet was thrown in as a compliment.

The lady was impressed with the two-year-old Vespa Elegante 125. She was happier to see the headlamp clad with the visor, the split seats were impressive, and moreover, the beige unico was the best choice. Her man might have felt she picked this because of the higher price, but only she knew the truth that the other VXL 149 scooter sucked in the sports red colour.

They decided to drive the new buy to Nandi Hills before returning home. While the guy did the driving through the mad traffic, the woman took over once the road ahead was clear. During the patches of the empty street, he moved his hands all over her. Ten kilometres away from the uphill, the scooter took a diversion to a secluded place. Three kilometres away from the main road, the duo found a large tree and no living life in the vicinity. Parking the scooter two hundred metres away, the duo took out the snacks they had bought on the way. Covered behind the tree for one-and-a-half hours until it became dark, the pair returned to the Elegante and got back to the city. Three hours down the road, the scooter was left in a 'Pay and Park' facility, eight main crossings away from Greenville.

5 PaPi Goes Live

The meeting of the official law holder in civilian dress and the criminals in their identifiable form took place in a dimly lit portico of a niche club in Indira Nagar. Police Inspector Dr Sripad Limbekai eavesdropped a surprise visit to Baja, and without the mafia's awareness, the policeman knew that the latter would be in the company of Jaani. The inspector was among the few people in the cosmopolitan city who knew the three notorious criminals by face. Baja correctly anticipated that the courtesy visit was bound to impose either more bribe tariff or restrictions in their movements, or both. He prayed for the lesser of the evils in a slightly more bribe tariff. In all cases, they would have to cough out twenty lakh rupees more by the weekend.

"*Sarkar! Phone kar diya hota*!" Jaani begged the man of law.

"Scotch!" Dr Limbekai ordered.

"*Jaroor, saheb*," Baja obliged.

Among all the tantalizing facets of the inspector, the least surprising aspect was his extra interest in the minuscule volume of the brisk panipuri sales. The inspector had a doctor of philosophy degree from Gulbarga University in a subject that's considered the toughest: Mathematics. He was not a pushover in the subject, and his scholar's degree was hard-earned with publication in international peer-reviewed journals. Hard-pressed, he could teach the tough arm of the subject in Functional Analysis with just two weeks of preparation. A keen eye in software programming, he believed that the next generation of surveillance lay in technology. He was also rumoured to have streamlined electronic bribe, among other crimes.

For the next fifteen minutes, the mathematician inspector enjoyed his scotch. He liked the dry-fruit starters provided in the club.

"You are not touching the next batch of engineers and entrepreneurs," the inspector informed them. Baja and Jaani were stunned, and the duo were at a loss over the verdict implied by the inspector. The blow was not yet complete for them. "And yes, you have the engineer in captivity, don't you? What's his name?" Dr Sripad looked at the two thugs, and continued, "Yes, Viraj Jain. Release him! Immediately."

Much before the near illiterates could comprehend the quantum of the order, the inspector left the club. Any diktat violation of the inspector meant encounter for the three, marking the end of the underworld crimes against the entrepreneurs.

PaPi! PaPi! PaPi! The Greenville housing secretary Romila Tagore went out of her way to get special permission allowing the young entrepreneur's team to flash little hoardings of the new enterprise across the allowable limits of the social club and a bit of the parking zone too. At a meeting of the society, she raised the request to allow a special screening of the PaPi in the club gathering. The love and pride of the secretary were rewarded with a sharp 5 p.m. ten-day supply of panipuri at her desk.

In the initial stages, ten delivery boys were hired on a part-time basis. To keep the costs lower, it helped the cause of Sagar Bansal that their prime time of serving was between 3 p.m. to 8 p.m. Coincidentally, the delivery boys of the regular powerhouses of Zomato, Swiggy, etc., are not that busy in this period. Sagar negotiated slowly and convinced the boys to work at the rate of three rupees per kilometre and a base of four thousand per month. A lot of the regular delivery boys saw the sense of making the extra money in their relatively free time. However, they were also clear that if in this duration, they get an order from their regular hirers, they would ditch PaPi. For every cancelled order after 7 p.m., PaPi promised to freely deliver a pack over the weekend.

A little angel investor pumped in ten lakh rupees a week before the launch, and Sagar was armed with enough artillery to make an announcement. Pamphlet distribution from Marathahalli to Silk Board junction was done generously, costing two lakh rupees. Flex printing, digital board advertisement, HSR News and EcoSpace Daily, Facebook and Google advertisements, etc., saw the burning of another six lakh rupees. Two lakh rupees were kept aside for the salaries of the delivery boys.

The initial bombarding of the new venture PaPi fired the imagination and the first week saw two thousand eight hundred orders placed over the app, and it fetched a revenue close to one lakh rupees. The cost of twenty rupees per order with the local vendors meant an approximate profit of forty thousand rupees. The delivery boys burned eight thousand kilometres, and that expense alone meant twenty-four thousand rupees.

Rudra made a claim that they needed to hit the mark of twenty thousand orders per week to see profits. Nobody contested his claims, and hence he did not have to justify his math. The six firmly believed to have momentum on their side and anticipated that three months down the line, they would hit the magic mark of one lakh orders and hence meeting the stipulation of those many orders would fetch them the VC's investment of $4,00,000.

The second week's cumulative order triggered a rude awakening. A little pattern was lost by the brilliant ladies of flat 1304. They controlled the data, and it was their jurisdiction to monitor sales growth. The first day had seen three-hundred and fifty orders placed. The second day it shot up and increased by nearly sixty-five per cent, and triggered five-hundred and seventy-five orders. The third day saw six hundred and forty sales and an increase of around twelve per cent. The three ladies were too lost in the dreams of having launched a successful enterprise and did not notice that the next four days had seen successive falls at the count of 480, 330, 280 and 145 orders.

The six did not observe the sharp decline in people's interest in PaPi by the end of the week, and every single day of the second week saw orders placed in two digits only. Rudra tried to dismiss this as a blip and backed the sales to shoot up. Koyal projected the sales timeline chart and that single representation demolished their confidence, setting off warning alarm bells. The mini angel's ten lakh rupees were burned entirely, and there was no going back to them with the request for more funds. Jim suggested pumping in the last of the reserves of two lakh rupees set aside for the salary of delivery boys in the advertisement.

"We certainly need advertisements, and that goes without saying. However, I don't expect to receive even the capital sum of two lakh rupees back, let alone the profits. Always remember, employees' salary money is never a source for the organization. Can you imagine what will happen to us if we don't get our salary for a single month?" Sagar ruled out liquidating the delivery boys' salaries.

The next two hours saw gloom and doom in the apartment. A million revival ideas were floated, and each of the ideas was smashed to the trash bin five times over. The six were undoubtedly running out of time, and Sagar took a thirty-minute break. He went out for a walk and roamed around Greenville and what he saw disturbed him immensely. Swallowing the bitter pill, he returned to the war zone and updated the team that in their anxiety nobody noticed that the billboards, flexes and other advertisement canvas had long been dumped in the trash bins. The cooperation from various stalls and other proprietors was based on an agreement that the displays would be kept for a week. Every single proprietor had volunteered to depict PaPi ads and encourage the entrepreneurs. It was a rude awakening twice over. The dismal orders should have been anticipated and not come as a shocker.

Scrolling over the inbox in despair, Sagar's eye fell on the communication between Koyal and www.pp.com. He asked Koyal without any reason, "Koyal, any idea of the traction we got because of pp.com?"

"Zero," Koyal said without a second's hesitation.

"Ah!" Yashashwini sighed in an I-told-you-so groan.

"Please spare me your 'I-told' look, Yashu. Zero not because it was hopeless traction. Zero because we did not avail that offer. The impact might still be nothing," Koyal added.

"Let's validate it all the same. We have nothing left to do," Sagar insisted on flashing the arrival of PaPi on pp.com. "Koyal, report facts. 'Three thousand five-hundred online PaPis served,' and we will see how it goes from there," Sagar had a hunch that he preferred to keep to himself.

Jim, Rudra and Yashashwini were firmly against the waste of effort in reaching out to pp.com. They argued that a fans forum was no big deal and they were better off preparing the presentations and other related activity to the venture capitalist. What they needed at the moment was money. Rathishree kept out of the deliberations and was too tired of the work behind the scenes. Though Yashashwini put her heart out in the scalability, her core engineering competency left a lot to be desired. Sagar tried to justify that there was already a VC on board whose stipulation of one lakh orders had to be strictly met. Trying to run behind another VC was to start all over again with unforeseen challenges. The three teamed up vociferously in their arguments, and by the time the debate was thirty-nine minutes older, Koyal backed their rationale. Sagar raised the white flag and said that he was giving them three days to chalk up an alternative strategy.

The three scarfed men met to deliberate on the conditions laid out by Inspector Sripad Limbekai. Tiku was appraised of the situation on mobile earlier, and he insisted on a meeting to decide the critical changes that had the potential to alter the course of their working.

"Viraj and his family are under my captivity after pulling a lot of strings and connections. I refuse to release him," Tiku shocked his partners with his decision.

When the authority of Baja was challenged, it was not for Jaani to defend it. The puzzle was all the boss's to solve. He would simply sit back and accept Tiku as his new boss if the current one was not competent enough. A small matter that wouldn't change was simple for Jaani. Baja was not his outright boss, and neither would be Tiku if things came to that juncture.

"Inspector Limbekai's orders are orders for you too. I am telling you to follow it. He will not repeat his order, he will execute the consequence of violating it," Baja was here to get things done.

"Baja bhai! Tell me one thing, why should I alone bear the cost of this endeavour?" Tiku was clear where this conversation was headed. Releasing Viraj had its own risks, and he would be at the forefront of the dangers. It was not optional to release Viraj, and then the threat had to be borne by all. He wanted compensation for the risk undertaken by him.

"Tiku! You have decided to extract your pound of flesh with this exchange. Out with your demands," Baja was patient.

"I will release Viraj, but I get to keep a tab on his family in Ahmedabad. This is non-negotiable. You have to take care of the cops' cost and risk for this. Also, I don't just lose Viraj, I lose the insights fed by him. We will be constrained, and there is no way we are going to kidnap another engineer. Jaani bhai has sixty per cent vendors, and I have the remaining forty. We swap the percentages, and for his loss in the numbers, he will get to keep the top-selling points, and also fifty per cent of my top selling points. I am reasonable, and you both know that," Tiku wanted to get a fair deal for losing the intelligence unit.

Baja was in a fix and yet he had to make a decision without a second wasted. "You are on," he declared, and this single decision shook their little crime world upside down. Tiku smirked, and Jaani did not frown on the injustice.

"I will release Viraj in two weeks," Tiku guaranteed. He finally got what he had been aspiring for a long time. The top-selling points could be turned around, and he knew how to do it. With a weakened Jaani, it would not be beyond his capacity to complete the takeover in five years. A major win for him!

Bang! Bang! Baja fired two bullets in under three seconds. The first killed Ramesh, and the second found the mark between Balwant's eyes. The two bodyguards were supposed to protect Tiku from all threats. Two new strong men came in.

"Jaani! Work with Tiku and keep all of your bestselling points. Take all of his best too. Give the shitty seventy per cent lesser points to him. The bastard is entitled to his rewards," Baja left the venue.

Baja knew there was no way he could ever let down Jaani, and Tiku had bitten more than he could chew. The grave mistake was to undermine his authority.

Sagar entered the bedroom in the evening with two cans of beer. While Rathishree was his girlfriend, melancholy seemed to be his wife since the morning analysis. The lady was busy with her office work. The embodiment of Captain Cool, the woman focused on the task at hand over the worry off her desk. Sipping her beer, she munched on some chips and continued with the assigned work.

Sagar did not waste his day either. He went over the neighbourhood all over again and assessed the scenario. In the afternoon intermission period, he met the delivery boys and took stock of their experience during the past two weeks. A few suggestions were useful, and he decided to incorporate them into the app and the delivery system. His next task was to meet all the panipuri vendors, and he figured out that they were content to receive their regular payment of twenty bucks per order. The steady vendor Alok was more forthcoming and reflected that his bosses had no beef with the online sales as their overall sales had no impact whatsoever. After the scrutiny of delivery boys and vendors, he next focussed the attention on the customers and conversed with forty of them. The online sales were enthusiastically welcomed by the customers, and except for the fear of getting fatter, everything was rosy for the end-user.

When money is the remedy, its dearth is the source of the issue. It does not matter how much of it is arranged, the demon at the other end will keep on increasing. The team's morale was down, and Jim and Koyal were very apologetic for not being able to reach out to more people on social media platforms. In a non-competitive spirit, Rathishree was finishing one after another task of the official assignments, and Sagar shot out email after email. A kiss to boot up the mood and do task Ax92 and write an email to VC2@fxy.in. Next – bug fix and four other bloggers successfully reached was celebrated with fondling and deep kisses by the chief entrepreneur couple. The pair knew to mix up things in the hottest manner and live up the night.

Four days after the depressing sales decline analysis, they saw a day-on-day surge in the traffic on the app and more engagement for the delivery boys. From steady three-digit sales over a fortnight, the daily sales reached a robust three thousand orders. The cash registers saw consistent ringing and Sagar was patient and did not reach out to the VC after reaching the target of one lakh orders. Instead, he waited for the mark to hit three lakhs, and four months later, shot the proposal. The rewards were worth the wait, and PaPi had an assured investment of a million dollars.

Gloom and doom to boom and dawn transformation miracles were pulled off by the leader. An all-week celebration was planned, and the signing on the dotted line for the VC investment was in the midst of the week. The six were enjoying a treat in the dining hall. When Jim expressed surprise at their change in fortune, Sagar attributed the success in a significant part to the support granted by the admin of www.pp.com. If the website had not flashed PaPi on the welcome and landing page, it would have been almost impossible for the enterprise to maintain steady sales. The scepticism of the cooperation of the fans' platform was not recollected to avoid the needless sour debates. The admin refused any financial benefits and was glad that the platform saved PaPi. Koyal asked if Sagar was able to make out the gender of the admin, and the negative answer triggered a wave of laughter.

The main PaPi couple ventured out of Greenville for a little walk and a little shopping. The fridge was running out of beverages, and undoubtedly there would be a shortage of favourite drinks when everybody graced the celebrations. Sagar took the list compiled by Rudra earlier in the day. The plan was to buy the groceries and confectionaries first, and the couple accomplished that. The next stop was the Madhuloka Liquor Boutique.

"Rathi, I can buy you two Greater Than gins," Sagar was delighted.

"I would have kissed you if we were in a car, or if you had promised this in the flat. Your loss, I guess," Rathishree laughed. The road was relatively empty, and it would be in full force a couple of hours later.

"A full gin Rathi tastes differently, and is intoxicatingly beautiful. I don't make too many mistakes these days," he winked as the two made their way towards Madhuloka.

"Absolut Elyx from my end for the PaPi turnaround. Cheers!" she raised the bar.

"Cheers!" he thanked her.

"I think we must be mindful of the expense all the same, and ..." Rathishree experienced a push from behind. She almost fell over but managed to keep her balance. However, the person who pushed her snatched her handbag. By the time the lady could gather herself, the thief had fled.

Two black bikes were roaring away in an adjacent street. The lady screamed, "Thief, thief," and Sagar gathered what was happening. The thief sped ahead and took a left turn. Sagar chased the thief and gained pace himself. When Rathishree took the left corner, the thief was a good eighty metres ahead, and Sagar twenty metres behind him. Suddenly, the thief crossed the road amid the light traffic. Sagar pursued the chase, and he too stepped on the road. The rogue wheelie on a black Activa automatic scooter cut in their direction. Before Sagar could move forward or backward, the motorcycle bumped straight into his chest and threw him violently fifteen metres away on the road. His head crashed on the asphalt violently and much before his body stopped rolling, another beige-coloured Vespa scooter ran over Sagar's chest. Sagar's head was split open with the impact and started bleeding. Sagar's broken body lay just three metres away from Rathishree, a testimony to the violent accident. By the time she reached him, over fifty people had gathered around them.

"Thief, ambulance" ... the shrieks continued all around, and Rathishree did not know what was happening. A few commuters tried to help with water. The bulging eyes told a different story. Long before the ambulance could come, Sagar was unconscious. Five minutes from the hospital, the last batch of air left his lungs.

An accident FIR was registered against the two wheeling rogues. Even though there was CCTV footage, the police were not able to arrest the ruffians. Sagar's parents flew in by the last flight and the next day took the body back to Vidisha and performed the last rites. The five, six minus Sagar, returned to Bengaluru after the final rites. Rathishree prepared to return to her native hometown in Hubli to recover from the shock. The PaPi enterprise came to a halt, and it was suspended until further notice.

"Rathishree! It is an unfortunate and devastating demise for all of us, and you, even more so. We are with you, and we are not going to give up so easily. As much as we know you are mourning Sagar, a few things still need very urgent attention. What happened in front of your eyes was not an accident; it was murder. As much as the police have refused to buy into the argument, we have arranged a press conference today. Please, for Sagar's sake, join us. It is important," Jim pursued.

"For Sagar. Thanks Jim, and Rudra, you too. I am really indebted," Rathishree appreciated her flatmates.

"The press-conference address begins at two. I guess you should still have plenty of time to catch the train," Rudra updated the time.

"One more request to both of you. Can you please address the media? I will chip in, but keep the dependency to a minimum. I will appreciate it," Rathishree was not yet in the reckoning to clear the media hurdle. The flatmates agreed, and at the designated time, all of them were present at the press conference.

"Mohit S, Sripathi F, Kaushik, Rodriquez M, and Anjali R! And now Sagar Bansal. Six entrepreneurs and all of them died in accidents. Road accidents. It is impossible to have so many coincidences, and hundred per cent of the entrepreneurs who tried to promote online sales of the simple panipuri have been killed in accidents. We urge the Bengaluru police to seriously investigate the criminal angle behind these accidents, and do justice," Rudra opened the press conference with a summary of their case. A well-wisher advised Rudra not to use the word "mafia" on his own. It was bound to be propped up by the media and journalists.

"Did you press for murder charges in case of your business partner Sagar Bansal?" asked a reporter from ABZ News.

"Yes, but the police have taken *suo motto* evidence and refused to press for a criminal offence, and dismissed it as a genuine accident," Jim said calmly.

"The police have experience. How can you not accept their version?" questioned a journalist from Kal Aaj Network.

"Please don't accept six deaths of the entrepreneurs as the evidence of the crime. But a hundred per cent elimination of those who have dared to enter the online panipuri sales forms the reason for our belief of the criminal hands behind this conspiracy," Jim added clarity. "How many entrepreneurs have to die to merit an investigation?"

"Do you think a mere panipuri mobile vendor will be the murderer of six entrepreneurs? Is it not far fetched?" wondered a media guy from the local and native TV 901 channel. The media not only knew how to trace a scandal, a crime, etc., but they were also quite capable of conducting the trial too.

"We are not saying an ordinary vendor is the murderer of our late colleague, we are only saying that this accident is highly suspicious. We are not fighting for our deceased friend, but for future entrepreneurs. Our fight is also for the better quality of life for the vendor, who is also a beneficiary of such online sales," Rudra presented a nuanced point.

"Do you feel the name of your enterprise PaPi, pronounced in the local dialect, meaning sin is a reason for the tragedy that has struck your deceased business partner Sagar Bansal?" wondered a reporter from a lesser channel. The lame argument triggered a wave of silly laughter in the press conference. Rudra and Koyal became furious over the ridiculous notion.

"We believe in rational arguments. Next question please," Yashashwini scored a good point for the young entrepreneurs.

"In our research, PaPi was on the verge of signing a million-dollar investment from a venture capitalist. The police, if it decides to investigate, might also suspect one of you five for being over-ambitious," the reporter from TV 901 tried to instigate the team of youngsters.

"We want the killing of Sagar Bansal to be investigated. We want the guilty killers of Mohit S, Sripathi F, Kaushik, Rodriquez M, and Anjali R to be identified and imprisoned too. If that means one or more of us are the conspirers, so be it. Arrest and punish the criminals and put an end to the killing of innocent entrepreneurs," Rathishree pressed for justice.

"Do you guys, or Sagar Bansal, suspect someone behind the killing of those five entrepreneurs?" asked another journalist.

"No, we do not suspect anybody in particular," Rudra put the five out of misery, and fast.

"Do you suspect the mafia who are often accused of controlling the mobile panipuri vendors to be the culprit behind the deaths of the six entrepreneurs?" a seasoned journalist enquired.

"We have no idea who the criminal might be. Our demand is for a free and fair trial," Jim answered the final question of the day.

The team dropped Rathishree to the railway station later in the day. Everyone hugged her in turns and assured her that she had their full support, and none of them would rest peacefully until Sagar's violators were firmly put behind bars. The media covered the deaths of six entrepreneurs in TV news, as well as the newspaper. A few headlines were amusing, "PaPi killer roams free," "Is the Mafia taking over the Entrepreneur world?"

The simple touch of him. The expressions were vivid when Rathishree wanted to simply go with the flow. How elegant and sophisticated was his forefinger on her lips. The lower ones, and though she had never realized it earlier, it marked the first time she was aware of the texture of her lips. Every single line and crossing appeared decorated as a wedding hall. There was no magnification of lips, and neither were any specialised biological cells transformed into sensors which were relaying her heart the distance of the forefinger. It appeared to her as though the finger was a giant UFO satellite landing on her lips. It was weird because he was an entrepreneur, and she was a rock-solid software engineer. Why would she dream as though she were a blushing teenager or a professional astrophysicist?

And then the counter strikers of the planet destroyed the alien's spaceship with a SCUD missile. Blood. Red. Red. Guts.

He was gone. Gone for good. Or rather, he was wasted for nothing. The return to the bedroom did not bring memories. They were home to the nightmare. The mentor, friend, lover and a great teammate. How many roles can one expect from a guy of merely twenty-four years? That accident which was nothing but a disaster. She knew it and anticipated it too. The same as him. Only, he was better in transforming the risks into advantages and outsmarted the last time to the point of no return.

She sobbed, not in sadness, but for the loss of the potential he had in him that sublimed into the empty space. She had to do something about the loss of her lover – to get back to his purpose, if not necessarily for vengeance. She could have forgiven the rogues over any other damage, but not this one.

Yawning and lazing in the queen size bed, with the memories of her emperor, Rathishree put her foot down on the floor and paused. She realized that she did not miss him at all, and certainly not until light is brought to the native home of the darkest tunnel. Jim and Koyal. Rudra and Yashashwini. The flatmates were in two minds over the unfinished work, and it had the potential to go either way. She could not have blamed them if they chose to go their independent ways and forgot the PaPi enterprise. The tragedy was hers, and it is not everybody who loses a partner at the beginning of their career. None of them had over two years of experience, and it would be naive to expect them to risk their career over a profound relationship. The other option was to retrieve the dreams. The dreams of impossibility laden with real danger. How could she not be grateful to them for standing with her?

The bitterness between her and the estranged friendly couple of Rudra and Yashashwini vanished like smoke under heavy rains. The support and the trust that they extended to her in reclaiming their lost dreams was a support that defined thick bonds. Sagar would certainly be smiling in the skies above their never-ending twenty-six storied apartments.

She got up and made her way to the bathroom, picked the brush and squeezed some paste on it. Always a fast brusher, she could not find the rhythm today. The bristles were either too hard on the gums, or as slow as a ghost compelled to sweep the shipyard. Two minutes to brush? She knew that her steps would be more time-consuming because she was weighed down by the burden of memories. She had to cut loose of the thick and hard chains, and she had to be patient. "Don't expect magic if you aspire to deliver engineering excellence," Sagar's wise sayings would return to her. Unawares, she used the tongue cleaner too, and after she rinsed it clean, the reflection of it belonging to him almost reduced her to tears. She had resolved not to shed a tear, and she managed to hold on to her resolution at least at this moment.

Turning the bathtub lever on, she went to the mini-table besides the bed. She had black coffee in the thermos. A habit of hers that was endorsed by Sagar must remain forever.

Inspector Sripad Limbekai summoned the lesser powerful mafias to another unusual club in Malathahalli. After sacrificing all the hot points of sales, Tiku Singh outrightly declined to be part of the sacrificial front and was ready to pay any price set by the head Baja and the now undisputed number two Jaani. The media carried the news the entire week over the presence of the mafia in ordinary mobile panipuri networks. Because of the sensation, the price would be twice the usual rate for the mafias, and they would have to make further compromises.

The inspector was enjoying his whiskey while Baja and Jaani were deposited in the opposite chairs. The two kept to themselves and bowed their heads in shame as errant boys do after the headmaster catches them teasing girls.

"I had told you bastards not to bother me on this front," Dr Sripad was seething in rage.

"It was not our work, we swear," Jaani confessed.

"We even told the boys to fully extend cooperation with the online sellers. It was additional business for us. Why would we kill that newbie Sagar Bansal?" Baja was more forthcoming.

"Have you brought the killer then?" the Inspector asked.

"It must be the handiwork of Sikander. He has his own boys spread across the city," Baja needed to pass the buck. The new competitor had been trying to find his foot in the mobile panipuri network, and yet hadn't been able to, despite being in business for nearly five years. Moreover, he was a much smaller fish, and even Tiku Singh would not entertain the prospect of Sikander indulging in foul play.

Dr Limbekai did not have time to dive deeper and interrogate the two oldies, and he drew out the revolver and unlocked it. The rogues did not have more than five seconds to think of the answer, and they chose the safer route.

"Sorry, sorry!" Baja regretted trying to divert the police personnel's path, "we have made the arrangements. Five crores, and the final stop. No more touching the software engineers and their online businesses. Also, we have brought three men who will confess to the crime – Jarokh, Mukesh and Rishabh. Keep them in jail until the matter cools off. Do whatever is appropriate with them."

The arrangements sufficed to put a lid over the sensational serial deaths of the entrepreneurs. Dr Sripad looked at the three offerings and felt their arrests would be satisfactory enough for the next few months. He planned to arrest Rishabh first. Three days later, his confessions would lead to the imprisonment of Jarokh and Mukesh. Six months down the line and depending on the dynamics of the case, he would let go of them, or kill one or two of them in an encounter. The inspector warned the heads that if any one of the big three of them tried to flee the city, their bodies would be floating in the gutter. The three wingless chickens were taken to a cheap hotel first, and then they were arrested as planned.

6 The New Neighbour's Dash

"The Patils moved out two months ago, and now we get new neighbours," Yashashwini relayed the information after fetching milk pouches in. Rudra was resting after an hour's workout on the treadmill.

"It does not take fifteen minutes to figure out that the new neighbours have moved in. Out with the details, Yashu," Rudra told his girl.

"Well, well, so you did not miss me for fifteen minutes, but looks as though you were looking through the door yourself. Sigh, I don't complain Rudra, do I? Now, as much as you pretend, you know about our neighbour, Josh Khandelwal. What I found in my fifteen minutes of Robert Ludlum investigation is that he is not a mama's boy like my boyfriend. The latter drops me like a hot potato whenever there is a hint of the great Damini's visit to 1304, Greenville. Josh has moved in with his girlfriend Veena Rao and momma Roshini Khandelwal. That's guts," Yashashwini spilt a few more beans. Damini was Rudra's mother.

The neighbouring flat had been under renovation for over a month, and the restructuring spared no expense. Rudra and Jim did their best to figure out the new neighbours, but could not get a whiff. The workers aside, even the manager of Rodriquez Interior had not been told about the new occupant's whereabouts. When they tried to lure the Greenville society secretary Romila Tagore to at least acknowledge the names of the fresh owners, she snubbed them big time. The mystery gave the impression that a hugely successful entrepreneur, a venture capitalist, CEO of a hundred crore company, or Directors of Fortune 500 companies might be the new neighbours. The name Josh Khandelwal did not ring any bells in any corner of the tech world. Rudra's first instinct on hearing any fresh name, since going the entrepreneur way a year ago, was to search for the profile on LinkedIn. The result for Josh was disappointing, and the lad had a mere one-year diploma course from IIM, Raipur.

"An early morning LinkedIn search with a dampener, hero," Jim mocked Rudra while depositing himself in the settee. "Koyal, the quick breakfast, please."

"Yeah man, I had huge expectations with all the exquisite restructuring of 1305. Turns out a dud *baniya* Josh Khandelwal has moved in it, and the only positive according to Yashu is that he has moved along with his mother Roshini, and girlfriend Veena Rao," said Rudra.

"Live-in partner, not a girlfriend. That's the more daring part, unlike you both chums who ask us to leave the scene at the mere hint of your momma's visits," laughed Yashashwini.

"Girls, love and pizzas. Don't you have anything better to think of, Yashu?" mocked Rudra. "Here, the men are disappointed at the middle-classness of the new neighbours, and all you can think of is the kind mother-in-law, or would be *sasuma*. We are even disappointed with Romila for keeping such a dud family a secret. Isn't it, Jim?" wondered Rudra.

"Did it occur to you to check for his mother Roshini Khandelwal on LinkedIn? I did, and here is the remarkable result. She is the Director of Business Loans, Yesso Bank. She might not offer bank loans to our panipuri venture, yet, but she might be the right woman to introduce you to the VCs." Jim rocked with his findings.

"I don't know about his mother Roshini. But his girlfriend Veena Rao can lure away our boyfriends as easily as the pied piper ran away with the boys to the woods. She's what, around nineteen. Look at this, Yashu," Koyal shared her mobile with Yashashwini.

"Wow! She has sent you a friend request on Facebook already? My guess is not even eighteen, and already live-in. Goodness, I am jealous," Yashashwini was surprised with Koyal's new online friend, "I wonder how she's traced you on the web."

"She's so umm, isn't she?" Koyal added.

"You were right about the boys. She's beyond terrific, and I would not trust them one bit hanging around her," Yashu agreed insecurely.

"Come on girls, we haven't yet seen her. But going by your feedback, I might already have a crush on this new dame on the floor," Jim laughed as Koyal handed over her mobile. Veena Rao was every bit the gorgeous damsel who could make anybody's girlfriend insecure.

"I have been sent a friend request too. Looks like a social media addict. What a beauty she is, Yashu. I must say, without prejudice, she is a hundred times more gorgeous than you,"

Rudra agreed with his girlfriend and already gave a negative vibe to her.

"Bitch, please! Frigging hells! She's twenty-seven and not the sweet eighteen of our guesses. Peep at her smashing resume on LinkedIn. A PhD in AI/ML from Harvard University under the guidance of the famous scientist Prof Robert Tobforest. If that was not enough, she's already got fifteen patents, ten publications and a BTech from IIT Kanpur in Computer Science. I am panting thinking of her achievements, and she is a mere five years older than me. Koyal, I am packing my bags and hitting the village. It is better to learn how to milk cows over the misbelief of retaining our boyfriends. See you, girl!" Yashu laughed at her perceived misery.

Veena Rao had apparently added all the five occupants of 1304 on social media. The next hour was quickly passed when the four were scrolling down the timeline of Veena's profile. She was with Josh for over three years, and they had spent over twenty holidays across different locales of the planet. Phuket, Lakshadweep, Jaffna, Singapore, Indonesia, Hong Kong, Paris, London, San Francisco, Goa and Rio de Janerio were some of the locations the couple had been to. Veena had quite a massive following on Facebook and Instagram.

The height of five feet seven inches augmented with four-inch heels put her at a tall five-eleven, and Veena Rao dwarfed and towered over her five-feet-four-inches boyfriend, Josh. The four flatmates chuckled at the little weirdity in the photos of the couple. It could not be denied that even barefoot on beaches, the man looked lesser than his woman. It appeared she owned him on every scale, and they wondered what she had seen in him to make him a lover.

Not just the four of them, the scrolling and scraping on the social media showed that all the comments were for the beauty and nobody even registered the presence of the beast. Josh was more handsome than most men, and he had the misfortune of being the boyfriend of the eye-catcher, Veena. The comments were a reflection of the attraction commanded by the beauty and the four of them conjectured that it wouldn't be long before she ended up with somebody else.

"No man can handle being ignored to this degree. Moreover, she deserves better," Koyal expressed the familiar feeling.

"She looks totally content with him. Seems he has already given her everything she wants. That's weird," Jim confessed.

"The audacity and the temerity! 'Sorry Yashashwini, I have to decline you on LinkedIn. Feel free to connect on Insta. Luv VR.' Does she mean we are not in her league to be connected professionally?" Yashu fumed.

"Doesn't that mean she rates her brain over her beauty? I thought it would be the other way round," Koyal said even as she was aghast too.

"Josh's accepted us on the professional network while his profiles wear a deserted look on the friendly platforms," Jim laughed at the contrast.

"The ugly beast has accepted us on all forms of digital platforms. A relief for the girls, I guess," added Rudra.

The next notification on Yashu's mobile was from their new neighbour Josh. "Don't mind Veena. She's fussy on the professional front and declined my request there too. Bye." said the message on Facebook Messenger.

"Hey girls, I have a brilliant idea. Why not invite the live-in couple for breakfast right now?" Jim threw a challenge.

"I can, though I have been snubbed. I have a condition of my own. If Veena creates a scene over the invite, not only will the doors of 1304 be closed on her forever, I will also be treated for the entire week with pizza. Game?" Yashu upped the ante, and the guys accepted.

'That's fine, VR. Can you both come over for breakfast? The Movers and Packers team can be trusted I guess :),' and Yashu shot across the message while her screen was also flashed on the mega TV screen. The idea was to see the live reaction of the gorgeous damsel.

'Not now, busy :)' came the reply from Veena.

'You can't be busy this soon,' and it was Koyal on the touchscreen now.

'Making love 🥰 ' flashed the reply after seventeen seconds. The four were confused.

'Prove it,' replied Yashu.

'For your eyes only, Yashu 😘' and then the live streaming started. The camera began with a view of the shower drizzling water, and then it moved down to her long, wet hair. The live broadcast of the gorgeous face with sparkling eyes reflected nothing but love. The four could not believe their eyes and wondered how long it would be before the camera went below the neck. Was she wearing a towel? Who the hell wears a washcloth under a raining shower? Was she even wearing a bra? Were they really getting hot? Why would she flash herself to rank strangers? Was Josh with her? Was she all nude? Amidst the questions, the camera streaming went offline with a concluding message, 'That's enough for a starter. Luv, VR. 🙈 '

"Wow, forget boys, she knows how to turn on a girl too," Koyal added after a low whistle.

"Don't read or see too much into it, Koyal. She's as straight as any of us here. If she was a lesbian, why would all of her photos be either with Josh or only with herself. She's just a little naughty," added Yashu.

"Why would she get naughty with you on live-stream and blunt with Koyal on the professional network? Things don't add up," grinned Rudra.

"She snubbed me on the professional network, not Koyal," Yashu corrected.

"Oh, come on! Don't hide it, Yashu, she's not sending those kiss emojis to any of us," Jim chipped in. A beat and three quarters skipped in Yashu's heart.

"Jim, Koyal and Rudra... See here, the wet hair and face with the very same emoji are there on Insta, created at this very instant. And look at the likes and love emojis under five seconds 💖 💕 ❤️ 💞 . She's a dashing beauty and a class of her own," Yashu's new findings put to rest all speculations. The four spent another hour scrolling through the profile of their new swanky, angelic, beguiling and captivating neighbour. As seductive and stunning a beauty that she was, her innocence and cuteness overwhelmed every other facet of hers.

As the live-streaming went offline, Josh could not contain his josh. Since the past three years when she had said yes to his proposal, Josh was never out of love for a single moment. It was unthinkable and a difficult compromise; he swore to never even think of not loving her. His mother was a mere two closed doors away, and the distance might be less than ten feet. When did he become so crazy for Veena that he did not allow worldly elements to stop him from making love to her? His thought went back to their first meeting even as he unwrapped her wet bra and took the rosy mound in his mouth.

He was in the fourth semester of MSc Math at the Central College, Bangalore University. A misogynist that he was, he continually teased his mother that men were superior. Roshini Khandelwal did great as a single mother, and she was highly successful, surpassing her own expectations. A self-made woman, she raised Josh herself even as her parents tried to persuade her to find a bridegroom two decades ago. They had one condition – that she should abandon her infant in an orphanage. Roshini kept these matters to herself until he came of age.

That sunny afternoon, Roshini asked her son to pick her up from All Day Coffee, Garuda Mall. He did not like the deviation a bit, and the excuse of her being busy with her client because of the meeting getting stretched did not cut ice with him. Cursing, he parked the car in the basement and took the escalator to the coffee house. Despite being in the vicinity, he called her again to confirm if he had to show up. He was getting late for his date with Medha.

"It won't hurt to spend a little time with the busy momma," Roshini answered her son, and bringing the call to an end, she responded to her client Veena, "Fussy. Very fussy and messy too. Boys are stupid, men as well."

"I don't know much about boys, or men," Veena said decidedly.

A boy was unabashedly staring at her, his mouth open. It was as though he was seeing a woman after being in a tin can for ten thousand years of captivity. Veena focused on her Blue Cafe and took several sips of it. The boy did not take his eyes off her and continued to shamelessly stare at her. She turned her attention to Roshini and spoke about their business. It took two more minutes to complete the formality, and Veena picked up her bag to leave. The bill would be footed by the banker, undoubtedly. "It has been a pleasure meeting you, Roshini ji," she said while rising.

"Thanks, Veena. It's a great pleasure doing business with you. Look at the irony, my son called me ten minutes back from the basement, and he is yet to reach here," Roshini said.

"Maybe he has reached and is waiting for you," Veena pointed towards the staring boy. The older lady turned around to find her son and blasted him for not joining them. She introduced the two of them to each other. Even in the presence of his mother, Josh did not take his eyes off the damsel. He smirked a hi, and the unknowing mother volunteered to drop the client home. Before she could reply, Roshini moved towards the parking zone. Josh approached the high-heeled beauty without any hesitation and audaciously gripped her wrist and whispered in her ears, "Let's go."

Roshini insisted that both she and the client needed to be chauffeured. He was further disappointed when Veena sat behind him in the Ford EcoSport, and that meant that he could not steal as many glances if she were sitting diagonally. Luckily for him, their apartment was first, and Roshini got down and instructed her son to politely drop the client, a friend's daughter, to her home in Malleswaram.

"I am not a driver," he cribbed. Veena got the clue and came to the front seat. Roshini had bid adieu, and the lass in the car was struggling to slot the seat belt. The belt had not loosened enough to reach the destination, and Josh saw the latch plate three inches shy of the anchor. He held the belt tongue and slid his hand over the webbing, slightly brushing her breast, and pulled the retractor. Stretching it, he fastened the lass securely in the seat.

The two-kilometre distance was full of traffic jams, and the bumper-to-bumper traffic allowed him to fix his eyes on her instead of the road ahead. She was not uncomfortable with his eyes locked on her, and since the time the two met, they were almost on her whenever it permitted, and often when it did not either.

"Why are you staring at me continuously?" she asked him.

"That's because you are unlike any girl I have seen," he told her.

"Don't you have a girlfriend?" she enquired.

"I had one till a few moments before I saw you," he flirted.

"What does that mean?" she thought he was kidding.

"I love you, Veena Rao," he confessed in the horrible traffic jam.

"You are lying, and you will go back to her behind me," she teased him.

"No Veena, I will never betray you," he was sincere.

"I did not allow you to call me by my first name," she continued to test him.

"You did not object either," he was even better. His mobile rang for the fifth time since they were together.

"Why are you not receiving your calls?" she asked.

"It is my ex's call. I had this special ringtone set for her. She does not matter anymore, and I am done with her," he was serious.

"If you are done with her, she deserves to be told that at the very least, isn't it?" she tested him with the thought that he did not have the guts to spill the bad news to his ex-girlfriend primarily because there was no bad news, after all. She could not be more wrong. Now, he called the ex-girlfriend back using the car's infotainment. Medha Gupta was the displayed name. The call was received on the first ring.

"Where the hell are you, Josh?" Medha asked.

"Oh, I am with my girlfriend, Medha," he declared as Veena's eyes opened wide. The little matter of punctuation was either not registered by the speaker at the other end, or she had not heard him properly.

"I am waiting for you at the college gate, your girlfriend is waiting." Medha giggled.

"I am done with you, Medha. I am with my girlfriend Veena Rao. See this," and he disconnected the call. He reconnected using a video call, came close to Veena, put his left hand around Veena's head and pulled her head on to his collar bone, and shot the message, "she is my one and only true girlfriend. I am done with you, and sorry for it Medha ..." and before he could complete saying Gupta, the call went dead.

"Hello, mister Josh Khandelwal! I am not your girlfriend, mind it," Veena protested while drawing herself out of his grip.

"Excuse me, you are certainly my girlfriend. I might not be your boyfriend," Josh corrected her.

"Yes, you are not my boyfriend," Veena agreed.

"I was not your boyfriend," he added.

"You were not my boyfriend," Veena agreed, and she had a hint of what she was getting into. Trouble. Love.

"I might not be your boyfriend right now," he rolled it off his tongue. He kept his left arm on her right collar bone.

"You might not be my boyfriend," she concurred with him.

"I might be, just might be, your boyfriend in the future," he slid down the hands on her thighs, and a moan escaped her lips.

"You might be, just might be, my boyfriend," she was careful with the trap. Now his hand went from her thighs behind her back.

"You are undoubtedly my girlfriend," he said as the traffic progressed by another inch, and his hands moved between her shirt and skin in the back.

"I am your girlfriend," she said without explicitly adding that it was according to him.

"You are my girl," he said quickly without any gap after her utterance.

"I am your girl," and caution skipped her altogether as his hands rolled from her back along the waist to her navel.

"I am your love," he said while circling the belly button.

"I am your love," she agreed as he tickled her navel fervently.

"I love you," he completed his announcement and took down his hand to her crotch.

"I love you," she agreed, and she indeed loved him by then. Now, she was looking at him continually while his eyes were focused on the road ahead. When she looked down, his hands were not there without a trace of being ever there. It was as if there was magic all around them, and she did not mind being his newest girlfriend. As her apartment approached, she did not realize when the car was parked in the secluded basement. When he turned off the headlight, it was darkness everywhere. Unbuckling the seat belt, he took his lips over hers and kissed her deeply. She loved his hand over her breasts, and after fifteen minutes of intimacy, he withdrew to his seat. She couldn't resist him anymore and moved over him, pressing herself entirely against his whole body and kissing him madly all over his face. A little below the chin, she stopped and invited him to her flat, and they went the distance. A year later, they started staying together.

Returning from the memories of falling in love with her, he fondly recollected how easily she came around to love him. She had not changed a millimetre in her appearance, a nanosecond varying in the heartbeat, and her magnanimity kept increasing by light years over the past four years. Most importantly, she never returned a kiss of his; she kissed him of her own.

She would never confess that she loved him the very instant she saw him, and she was more capable of transgressing the love with him than the other way round. He might have seen her the first time with the speed of light; hers was with the speed of love.

"Gandu, band kar teri online dukaan, warna tikne nahi dunga Bangalore mein," the anonymous caller blasted the warning as the mobile greeting. The revealing words were pronounced as soon as Rudra said "Hello!" after receiving the call. He said hello a couple of times and the line was already dead. 'Private Number' was the display when he got the call on his mobile. He regretted receiving the anonymous call, and after the threat was received, there was little he could do about it.

The strategy of pressuring the police department through the press conference and social media worked. Jim insisted on putting their grievances on www.pp.com and more than fifty thousand followers shared the post on social media. The hashtags of #SaveEntrepreneurs, #SavePoorMobileVendors, #OnlinePuris, etc. trended on Twitter. After Rathishree left for Hubli, a sub-inspector paid a visit to their apartment the next evening. He came along with two constables and discussed the issue for over two hours. He also spoke to Rathishree over a phonecall for close to half an hour. The arrest of three panipuri mobile vendors over four days also showed the effectiveness of the Crime Branch, and Inspector Dr Sripad Limbekai personally assuaged their fears and encouraged them to carry forth their deceased friend's enterprise.

Rudra had two ways to go forward, regarding the threatening call. The first was to appraise the others of the threatening call – 'Five for One' and 'One for Five' spirit. He did not like the anticipated reception of the threat by the team.

They were recuperating from the death of Sagar, and another series of warnings would take away all the motivation. Series! Oh, it is just the first, and he had already exaggerated it to a series. He did not like that the most resilient member of the team, meaning himself, had such negative vibes, and hence deferred appraising. The second way was to keep the threat to himself. This strategy too had a dangerous fallout. What if the murderer was out for any of them and not necessarily marked only him? Was he not responsible if something went wrong with the others? Two ways to go forward and both were laden with high risks.

When Yashashwini returned from the grocery shopping, his face was pale, and she could not help being worried. He assured her that it was nothing more than a fond memory of their mentor pal. Was she convinced? He was happy to see her hitting the kitchen, her doubts being rested. But fear lingered in his heart, and every time he unlocked the smartphone, his impulse was to check if somehow the 'Private Number' revealed its correct ten digits.

"Pizza time at VJ! Come over at 7 p.m., please." The new message read after it was opened on the very informal MobileChat group of the neighbouring couples "LOVE 130504". It was a surprise invite by Josh in the group formed by his girl Veena. Koyal and Yashashwini were not sure whether to accept the invite or not. Jim chided them for overthinking and replied affirmatively on behalf of all the flatmates. He was of the genuine opinion that the new neighbours might have been busier earlier in the day with the unpacking and settling down.

Josh checked about the nonresponsive fifth member, Rathishree. To that end, the Hubli lady herself replied, urging the guys to carry on as she was busy with a close relative in the city, and she had other individual businesses to fix up. The new neighbours were sensitive regarding the demise of Rathishree's lover.

When the dynamic four pressed the bell and waited for the door to open, they read VJ on the board. When the door opened, the hostess took the breath away. The gorgeous Veena Rao was countless times more ravishing and seductive in appearance than in her photos and that sultry mini video. A controlled but irrepressible low whistle escaped from the lips of one of the visitors. The host asked them to grace their home. The vibrant imitation paintings of the Ajanta caves were displayed in the short corridor. A pair of finches in a small rectangle cage hummed melodiously. The interiors of the refurbished flat were beautifully done in the main hall. Sandalwood furniture and carvings could be seen everywhere. The sandalwood brown and the dusk black artwork were nicely mixed throughout the room, delivering a rich and luxurious experience. At the gap of every two-and-a-half feet, a man-sized digital display of the gorgeous Veena was depicted unabashedly.

"That is Josh's way of embarrassing me. The original idea of the digital displays was to depict sages and god's photos, and exotic nature's beauty at other times. He was monitoring the contents through the laptop, and that's his way of shaming me. Welcome," Veena sighed.

"I am sure you would already know our names through Facebook. Even then, I am Koyal Mehra," the Uttar Pradesh lady extended her hand in greeting.

"I am Yashashwini, also fondly called as Yashu. I am from Maharashtra," the Marathi girl not only greeted her with a handshake, but extended the introduction to a hug too. Veena then firmly shook hands with Jim and Rudra.

"Where is Josh? And also, the senior lady?" Jim was curious.

"Josh has gone out to drop his mother to their home in Malleshwaram. He will pick up the pizzas on his way back. He should be here any time now. Make yourselves comfortable," Veena asked the neighbours to relax.

"Hey, Yashu! See, all your talks of momma's boy flak of us turn futile," Rudra said.

"Oh no, that was not her construction. Roshini aunty had half moved here. An emergency return to visit her parents in Rajasthan compelled an unexpected trip. She will be joining us as soon as she can. Yashashwini got the information from the horse's mouth when she paid us an early morning visit. I did not see her then," Veena gave away the information that had been hidden by Yashashwini. Her flatmates were astounded, and they were careful not to let the new neighbour know.

"Why don't you tell us more about yourself? I guess, we would benefit a lot with your journey thus far," Yashu asked the host.

"I am a boring person. Josh is the superstar who can salvage you from any dull moment," Veena did not try to be modest. She did not have any opinion about herself.

"Modesty must be propelling you then. We are all too cocky about our little achievements. Please Veena, there is a sea difference between us. You can hold it until he comes," Koyal was also enthused with the host.

"I guess once Josh returns, we can know more about their love story. Until then, please Veena, give some gyan over your career progression," Jim was also interested in the details.

"For instance, you did your Ph.D. in a record time of two years. Was it not with the famous Prof Robert Tobforest? How? It just blows away the mind!" requested Koyal again.

"Love's the reason for the fastest Ph.D. in my case," Veena giggled. She served the guests with mocktails and sat on a settee herself.

"Wait! Let me guess. You finished your Ph.D. approximately four years ago, and Josh was still pursuing the close of Bachelor's degree or the first year of Master's. You could not keep away from him for a long time, and so wrapped up the research in record time, isn't it?" Yashu was fast in her insights.

"I had not met Josh three years ago. It is also a bit mysterious that we were in love a long time ago, almost as if in a previous birth. Let's keep away from Josh's story. I actually fell in love with the assistant professor at Boston. Dr Steve McLachlan. He was also a Ph.D. student of Prof Robert Tobforest. Because I was in love with Dr Steve, I blindly did everything he told me to. The research kind of automatically took care of itself. In fact, Dr Steve visited India for a month too. Unfortunately for me, though he loved me too, it was of a different kind. My face, this very disgraced face, LoL, was the same as his daughter's, and I reminded him of his kid. He is still very fond of me, and I still love him. A love of its own kind and merit. So, you can see, there was nothing genius about my Ph.D., ha, ha."

"Wow! You have proved that love can help you become a genius too," Koyal gave a thumbs up to the charming beauty.

"Are you sad at the way the love saga ended for you?" wondered Jim.

"No, it was possibly the best finish. Love can't always be about yourself. Dr Steve loved me ever since my photographed application reached the university. When god decides your fate, how can you deny the truth," Veena became emotional about the small story, and later requested her new friends to drop the topic.

"In terms of sheer geniuses, I had the fortune to meet the iconic scientist Dr Indian Scientistwala Kanference. She was a visiting professor during my IIT days. She took me under her tutelage, and there has been no looking back. I owe more to her and Dr Steve for my research motivation. Even Prof Tobforest respects my view. Do you know that the great professor has offered me a permanent position in his department whenever I am tired of the IT job," Veena blushed like a teenage girl. She looked like a teenager too.

"I have read a lot regarding Dr Indian Scientistwala Kanference. The weirdity around her name, the humble background, the struggle to become a scientist, etc. It is overwhelming to know about you, Veena, and I can get an impression of what it is like to be mentored by the likes of this great lady, and Profs Tobforest and McLachlan," Jim was mighty impressed.

"Academics suck, don't they?" Yashu played spoilsport.

"Certainly! If they keep you away from love," Veena laughed. The chatting veered towards the other pairs' love stories. She was splendid in discovering the forthcoming engagement of Jim and Koyal. She agreed that Yashu was too raw to consider serious commitments. The hostess did not register a pair of blink free eyes locked on her face since the door was opened.

Josh joined the apartment with the bag of pizzas. Potato wedges, brownies and coke were the other companions of the pizza in the bag. The hosts did not ask for any choice of the flavour and took it on themselves with the order. Preparing the serving plates, Veena updated her lover over the discussion that unfolded until his arrival.

"Congratulations! How long have you been together?" Josh asked Jim and Koyal.

"Around six months. Four for Rudra and Yashashwini. Yourselves?" Jim asked the hosts.

"Three years. Not in any hurry for the nuptials," Josh giggled. He got up to get the cold drinks while Veena returned to the seat and engaged the neighbours.

"Are you fine with it, Veena?" Yashashwini wondered.

"Perfect! We are not thinking of marriage," Veena said assuredly. The chips packets were passed from one to another.

"Apologies if it is too much to ask in the first meeting. We saw your Instagram wall, and you have been all over the world. What's holding you back?" asked Koyal.

"He never asked" and "she never asked" were uttered simultaneously by the hosts. Laughing, Veena got up from the couch and hugged her boyfriend. "Who initiated the proposal in your case?" asked Josh to Jim.

"He" and "she" was now the one-word answer said in unison by the couple waiting to get committed. The hosts continued laughing, and then Veena pointed to Yashashwini about their plans.

"No," and there were no two different answers from this couple. The Rudra-Yashashwini duo was left red-faced.

"How can you say no, Rudra?" Yashashwini was furious.

"You said the same, no. Stop being a hypocrite," Rudra counterattacked in a rage.

"My no meant not different from them. Facial expressions mean a damn thing or two. Your 'no' clearly said you are not serious about the relationship. Everybody could see it plastered on your face," Yashashwini twitched her lips, expressing her fury.

"Team, team, team. Boys and girls, men and women... let me open the pizza boxes," the hostess volunteered. Her intent was obviously to stop the feud from escalating and ruining the elegant evening.

"What's the hurry?" wondered the handsome Rudra.

"My guess is we were delayed by Josh's getting the pizza. Besides, I have a few meetings to attend to, and honestly speaking, I am hungry too," Veena opened the pizzas of different types and arranged them in five plates. The neighbours wondered for a moment if Josh was fasting. After four plates were filled with pizza, wedges and brownie, they were handed to the neighbouring couple, and then Veena sat on Josh's lap. They took turns feeding each other. The VJ couple led the way in depicting their romance in the unabashed style developed over the years.

"Rudra! Why are you nervous?" Veena asked out of the blue. She asked after Josh murmured in her ears.

"No, not really," Rudra was taken aback by the sudden remark, and quickly stashed the mobile back in the pocket.

"Something's the matter, and I feel it definitely. It is the sixth time in the last fifteen minutes that you take your mobile out, unlock it, check for something on your mobile, your face turns pale, and then the mobile goes back into the pocket," Josh remarked.

"Oh, nothing, it is just the alerts. Six checks under fifteen minutes are quite normal," Rudra smiled. But he could not sell it to anybody.

"Six in fifteen, not much so. Eighteen out of thirty is a hell lot. Besides, you are getting weird kinds of alert notifications. Neither your mobile is on vibration mode, nor a volume alert is giving away the warning. Heck, you can't have eighteen of the same kind of alerts. Be home, tell us," Josh was more forthcoming. He reflected honest concerns.

"No, nothinggg," Rudra pretended to be lucid.

"Wait! What's the matter?" Koyal too persisted. The coercing did the trick, and Rudra confessed to getting a threatening call. The matter was grave, and the threat of the anonymous caller could not be ignored. Veena asked Josh to fetch her personal laptop and the Android USB cable.

Connecting Rudra's mobile with her laptop, and running the history of the calls received, Veena used CocoSpy007 software to determine the GPS location of the mobile that made the call. It took her seven minutes as the 'Private Number' posed several challenges.

"Seven hells! Josh," Veena was shaken to the heels. She was almost on the verge of a breakdown.

"What's the matter? Where did the call come from? Whose mobile was it?" Rudra asked.

"It is disturbing, friends. The call was made from our little verandah, near the cage of the two finches. And ..." Josh was genuinely perturbed.

"And what? Was the call made from your mobile, or Veena's?" Rudra turned furious with the revelation that the new neighbours were home to the threatening call.

"Well, it was made from… from Koyal's mobile," Josh's revelation silenced everyone.

"Koyal's?" Jim was shocked.

"It must be a software bug. What nonsense is this?" Rudra was disturbed.

"Veena! Is this a joke?" Koyal was furious too. She looked intimidatingly at the host.

"Look, guys! You can run your other mobiles' history with the software and confirm the location yourself for different times and calls. Why will a technology lie? I ran the program multiple times, as it does not take more than a minute to run. Please, test for yourselves," Veena offered clarity.

A full hour was spent on testing the presence of the different mobiles and different locations, for varied times. Every single result was picture perfect. The results of calls from even a month ago were unmistakably correct. There was no reason to disbelieve why the threatening call's location and mobile number will be false information.

"Do you have CCTV footage from around the time of the call?" asked Jim.

"No, unfortunately, our systems are not going live until the coming Thursday," Josh revealed.

"So, it has to be one of the guys from the movers and packers. He must have taken out Koyal's mobile from our flat, come to that corridor, and made the call as a Private Number. We can get the footage from the society's camera. It should not be difficult," Rudra was pumped to do the spy work.

"We had a power failure around that time. So...." Yashu added.

"Guys, sorry. I need to rush to a meeting," Veena stormed out to her little office within the home. She instructed Josh to attend to their neighbours.

The six were reduced to five, and Jim almost felt sad about the silly observation.

"Dry throat. Beer?" Rudra asked.

"I am sorry, guys. This is a teetotaller's home, and as such I regret not inquiring for your preference of veg/non-veg for the pizza because that's not allowed either," Josh was apologetic for the little letdown.

"Smoking?" Jim desperately needed a drag and two.

"I need beer as well as a cigarette," Josh was clear of his requirement.

"Ah! The mice come out to play while the cats are away. So, she's your boss, Josh?" Koyal said smugly.

"The boss who will work for you! The truth is always the bitter pill to swallow. Now, can she really help with office meetings if she draws the salary of a twenty-years experienced specialist? I guess no. Besides, you will not like attending her meetings because it is technical shit of math, formulas, AI, stat and other monsters. Fuck that. I have beer cans in the car. Let's go to the parking zone," Josh solved the more critical complex problems of the world.

"Ah! We have plenty of that in our fridge. 1304 is not a bad place to live in," Koyal offered to swap the roles of guest with the host. The next three hours were the best of the week. When the stock of seven cans was over, it made sense to fetch some more from the parking.

PaPi thanks PP, An Ode to Sagar Bansal: The Creator of PaPi, No Discussions on Sweet Panipuris, The Rainbow of Puris, What's New in the World of Water Pancakes, etc., dominated the discussions in the fans' forum www.pp.com. Rudra and Yashashwini voluntarily deleted their accounts on the website after the ugly fiasco of creating a thread on the portal became controversial. The correspondence was handled by Koyal and Jim. Though Rathishree still had access to Sagar's online account, the ID was deactivated.

Viraj Jain struggled to come to terms with the almost unconditional release by his captors. He was the sole witness to the rogues who controlled the panipuri world in Bengaluru. Yet, he had not seen them even once. He was starved during the first three months of being kidnapped. Physical assaults were not as vicious as what he witnessed Tiku Singh unleash on the hapless vendor boys. How does one measure the fear-factor trade-off between physical abuse and the threat that any member of the family can be killed? When Tiku released him without any financial exchange, he was surprised. The happiness was short-lived when Tiku revealed that there were tabs on his family in Gujarat. Another solace came in the permission to visit his family.

Two months after his release, he managed to secure a job in a small start-up company in Gurugram. He did not know how to get his family wholly relieved from the clutches of the mafia without using the police. After being clueless for a significant period, he was back to watching porn in the incognito mode.

And as he got a few pings on the MobileChat, he closed the dark browser. After the conversation was completed, he opened the incognito mode yet again, the change in practice hit him back, and he laughed at himself. In captivity, he was watching porn in the regular browser and checking emails in the incognito, and now it was reversed. Oh, hold on!

Why was he checking emails secretly? Two very near identical IDs, oh yeah. PPwala and PPwila. The first id was for Tiku Singh and the second for himself. Yes, that was it. He could have been helped by the admin of www.pp.com, and he needed to first connect with him.

Message 1: *The bird is free. The bird's family still in the cage.*

Message 2: *The first vowel is Hunter's.*

Message 3: *Can you help? No matter how much little you can help.*

It was a lucky day for Viraj, and the reply came instantly.

Reply to Message 1: *Congratulations. Really happy for you. Don't risk your family.*

Reply to Message 2: *Account deactivated.*

Reply to Message 3: *Hunter needs to be hunted. You need to trust us for help.*

That was enough for Viraj, and he was delighted to know that the admin/owner was ready to help in his limited capacity. In the earlier phase, he wanted to desperately communicate home and draw some solace. He conveyed a little story from childhood to the admin and shared his home contact number. The admin got back to him with another childhood narration from his family.

He was convinced he could go ahead with the details of the mafia with www.pp.com.

Message 4: *I do trust you. How do we go about it?*

Reply to Message 4: *What's the structure of the mafia world?*

Reply to Reply to Message 4: *I was kidnapped by a head called Tiku Singh. I thought he was the main head. Four months later, two more joined with the names Jaani and Baja. One of them is the head for sure, and the other two are the chiefs, no idea who is who.*

Reply to Reply to Reply to Message 4: *Can you sketch their faces?*

Reply to Reply to Reply to Reply to Message 4: *No. Unfortunately, the three would always cover their faces with scarves.*

Reply to Reply to Reply to Reply to Reply to Message 4: *How can the three be reached then?*

Reply to Reply to Reply to Reply to Reply to Reply to Message 4: *Every panipuri mobile vendor leads directly to either the two of them.*

Reply to Reply to Reply to Reply to Reply to Reply to Reply to Message 4: *Do they carry a mobile? Gun?*

Reply to Reply to Reply to Reply to Reply to Reply to Reply to Reply to Message 4: *Always. No.*

Reply to Reply to Reply to Reply to Reply to Reply to Reply to Reply to Reply to Message 4: *That helps. The earlier favour of calling your home was a simple task. Don't keep high expectations. I am a mere software engineer and not a strong military man. Ok, bye for today.*

Viraj did not delete messages from the PPwila account for the first time.

Four months ago, Kamali and Barfi were taken forty kilometres away to a large five-bedroom house villa near Bannerghatta Road. The villa society was eight kilometres away from the main road. On the day the duo was dumped in the outhouse, a manager told them to keep the garden around the villa clean. They were provided with a lovely furnished two-hundred square feet studio home. Early in the drive, the driver asked the duo to throw away their mobiles. Barfi confronted that his family numbers were in the mobile and not in his memory. The driver said the other option for him would be to kill them.

The owners had visited the holiday villa three times since their stay. Every time, they had to sweep and mop the villa half a day before the arrival. The good part was their efforts were never wasted. The manager gave them a combined salary of ten thousand rupees a month. The food provisions were supplied in the third week of the month. Barfi mustered courage and asked what would happen if the duo fled. The manager said it was their wish and there were no compulsions. The offer was simple. Maintain the garden neat and clean daily. Tidy the villa a day before the owners' visit. Their reward would be ten thousand rupees a month and the monthly provisions.

Barfi was happy with the new scheme of things. He was not too worried about his family in Manihari, and Kamali was already independent. If his independence was the sacrifice at the expense of his parents, he was sure they would be happier with his decision. Besides, this choice was almost a compulsion in the beginning. The couple was delighted even as they were not married.

"What's the need of marriage?" questioned Kamali.

The daily garden maintenance did not take more than three hours of their time. The only other task they had besides sleeping and cooking was making love. Barfi was disappointed that though they were having sex almost twice a day, he was not able to impregnate her. He was not too worried otherwise. A lovely afternoon, the flowers of the garden were blossoming elegantly, and the two were relaxing on the porch. The gate opened. A bike drove in, closing on them. The biker took a turn and parked instantly and parallelly to the porch, and got off the bike walking towards the couple.

The dreaded RX-100 bike and the biker with a full-face helmet sent shivers down the two spines. Kamali and Barfi were getting up when the biker waved at them to sit down and relax.

"Don't worry, you are free," the biker said in a heavily machinated voice. The hideous jacket and biker's complete safety gear did not reveal the gender. Even in the dreaded state, Kamali felt that the biker could not be a man. Why would a man hide his voice? She asked herself and deduced the biker must be definitely female. At the same time, Barfi was convinced that the biker must be definitely male because the villa was as far away from society as it could be. A female might be able to drive a bike like RX-100, he did not question that, but would she be safe from the hawks. For instance, he would be able to force two women if he wished, and there would be no safety for them. The machinated voice was definitely to disguise the original sound.

"Barfi!" the biker summoned, "Who was your *malik* at Wadarbandyapalya?"

"Jaani!" he answered. Clearly, he regretted thinking of the biker as a female. Even if the biker was a female, he was better off from the dangers of returning to the turbulent and cheap mafia world.

"Who is above Jaani?" asked the biker.

Barfi had to think hard. Jaani was definitely reporting to somebody, and who might that be. Yes, the day Shikhan was caught by Jaani, a call went out from his mobile to the main head. "Baja," he revealed the super boss's name.

"Would Jaani call you on your mobile?" asked the biker.

"Yes, at least once in a week. Are you turning us back to the mallik? If yes, please spare Kamali," Barfi was in tears. He could not bear it if Kamali had to be part of the sinister world.

"No. You are free," the biker granted liberty. Returning to the motorcycle, the single-kick put life back in the engine, and the bike sped away.

"Can you join for tea?" popped up a message in the afternoon on the MobileChat group LOVE 130504. Rathishree posed the question to Veena Rao, and it was the fourth day since the newly furnished flat was occupied.

"For sure, if it suits you," Veena shot the reply, and the two were sitting across the table twenty minutes later. The rest of the flatmates were at their respective offices.

"A much overdue visit, residing two doors away," Rathishree stated the obvious.

"Near, but nobody is free," Veena agreed.

"Koyal and Yashashwini are gaga over you, and you are truly a very down to earth person. How are you allowed work from home for four straight days? My manager never grants more than a day per week, and two in a row is strictly forbidden," Rathishree wished to know.

"You mean boss and not a manager. Bosses are not kind, and I have a manager as my higher-up. When I put in my papers to take a year or two off from work after a year's stint at AT&B Finance, New York, the manager asked for the reason. I had enough savings because of the dollar to rupee exchange rate, and I missed my momma a hell lot. Three years away from her was too much. I was dying to return and be with her. The manager then granted me the 'Work from India' option as the company does not have a branch here. I need to spend June and December in the New York head office, though. The same dollar salary and fully paid half-yearly airfare were too lucrative a deal. I grabbed it with both hands and legs. So, here I am," Veena gave away the status quo.

"And then Josh's love happened too. Am I right?" Rathishree asked.

"Yup! Three months ago, my father took retirement for good, and now he takes care of my mother. She needs more care after her second heart attack. So yeah, the jigsaw puzzles fell in the right places, and here I am," Veena smiled. Her flatmates were damn right, the host reflected unto herself. The smile would kill a million lovers. She was not herself immune from that infectious simper.

"Your boyfriend Josh purchased the apartment. There can't be a worry in the world for you, isn't it?" Rathishree was doubtless happy for the neighbours.

"Oh yeah! You can say that," Veena flashed her glorious smile in confirmation. She wondered why Josh had lied to impress the neighbours.

"I have been trying to fix a bug related to the real-time location synchronization over the past three days. Yashashwini and Rudra too tried their hands at fixing the bug, and yet we are not able to fix it. We are all thus stunned with your abilities. Take a bow, Veena," Rathishree praised her.

"I can try to help you with the issue, if you don't mind," Veena offered to help.

"No, no, I didn't mean to trouble you at all. We will fix it one way or another. No problem," Rathishree was hesitant to needlessly bother Veena.

"Josh told me that you have together created a wonderful app called PaPi. I like the pun it implies. Are you sure that I can't be of help? I have seen that many times people don't take help because they are sure of the other's lack of capability in solving the problem," Veena laughed.

"No, I can't doubt your abilities at all. It is just that you are now in the AI/ML universe," Rathishree was positive over the non-requirement of the extended support.

"Rathishree, I respect your decision, and it is your world. I have no doubts that you will fix the issue. But don't forget that I have a Computer Science degree from IIT, Kanpur. I am just twenty-seven and not yet too dated not to follow the app bugs issue," Veena was not too adamant, and yet she wanted to really have a go at the issue.

"Are you sure? It will take me at least an hour to simply take you to the issue," Rathishree felt that lack of time might help propel the guest to withdraw from the voluntary help.

Veena checked the time. She had two hours and felt that it would be shameful if she did not try to resolve an engineering issue. Reluctantly, Rathishree brought the laptop and tried to explain the setup from scratch. Veena stopped the younger engineer and said that she understood all of those details and the installation. She insisted on being taken directly to the code block of the live-location synchronization bug. Rathishree tried informing her that the technical steps could not be skipped, and Veena gave a 'don't-insult-me' stare. Now, instead of Rathishree walking through the file block, Veena used the local search and dug out the file which had codes related to the synchronization bug. She opened it and looked at the lines, and the settings used by the developers.

"Ah! There you go. See, you have jumbled the options for ACCESS_COARSE_LOCATION with ACCESS_BACKGROUND_LOCATION, and that's the problem. Here," Veena changed the settings, and that resolved the problem.

"Was that all the beef with it?" Rathishree was stunned.

"Yup!" Veena solved the problem. It was not even ten minutes since the session started.

"Wow! You are stupendous, Veena. Truly remarkable. Are you not tempted to go the entrepreneur way?" Rathishree wondered.

"Not really! Especially after seeing what you guys are doing. I mean, don't get me wrong, I really regret Sagar losing his life this way. But seriously, are you guys putting technology to good use for selling panipuri? Is that all you can think of?" Veena was aghast with this kind of engineering application.

7 The Burst of Crispy Pancakes

Alok moved the mobile unit to the usual location at HSR Layout. He knew about the death of Sagar Bansal, and he had not seen the mafia boss Jaani since that accident. The murmur among the hapless vendor men was that any of them could be handed over to the police as the head mafia. The fear was not unfounded as they were aware of Jarokh, Mukesh and Rishabh having been handed over as the sacrificial goats to please the society's thirst for justice. Did he wish for the death of the entrepreneurs? Far from that. However, he did not appreciate his fellow companions, wherever they might be, to end up in prison for no fault.

Normally, in the first hour he would have no customers. Alok took some tobacco leaves from his pouch and added some lime to it. He started rubbing the lime on the leaves. "*Dus rupayye ka kitna,*" asked the familiar voice of the streetwalker.

"*Bohni nahi huyi, aur aa gayi,*" Alok was annoyed with the bitch turning up before the first sale of the day. The hooker was a known and familiar entity for Alok.

After Barfi fled from the unrelenting claws of Jaani, the night ended in a massive beating for Jarokh, Bholu, Ghumroo and him. The crowbar was unleashed at least ten times on their backs. To this day, there had been no trace of Barfi. He turned away the hooker Reshma every time she showed up since Barfi's disappearance.

The professional hooker Reshma knew how to work her way around men's hearts. The girlfriend gets her place by accessing the heart while the wife earns her spot through the stomach. The hooker works her way through a few inches below the belly. She knew her work around a seller who had not yet got his *bohni*. It was common for her to trade a kiss or two for a week's share of the panipuri. He was putting her off for over two months, and yet she would not give up trying. Today, lust got the better of him.

"Go behind the grass. I will join you in five minutes," Alok told Reshma.

"Babu, I want you to pour down the hardest today," she wanted more, way more.

"I sell panipuri, not jewels. No way can I commit a full month's supply. Look somewhere else," Alok did not want to take such a huge risk for an hour's happiness. In contact or not, Jaani and the others did have their eyes on them all the time.

"Fourteen months! We have known each other for a long time. I don't want money. Please understand your needs, Alok," the hooker persisted.

The warmth got the better of desperation this time, and Alok gave in. "I will take an hour off for you. Take the next left and wait for me. I will ask Seth to look at the puris for an hour," Alok asked her to wait for two minutes.

With the instructions to look after the mobile unit addressed, he purchased a condom from the medical shop. Alok was thrilled to rejuvenate the spark after a long time. It was over a year since he had entered the deep caves, and there was an opportunity beckoning. He had kissed Reshma on six occasions, and when she was in prime, she was pricey too. A slip of hands on the mounds meant an extra hundred rupees. He almost ran towards her, and then the two moved away taking quick strides.

"Where?" he asked for the location, and her response of "The roof of Greenville" shocked him, and then followed her explanation. "I have regular customers there."

He smiled, and she elbowed him in the belly, "I am taking you to a pricey location." The risk of being caught by the police did not arise. The proof in the pudding rested when the security did not question her entry at all. They did not even bother to enquire about Alok.

Reshma took him to a servant's quarters on the roof. She asked him to first clean his hands in the sink. She took off her top and lolled like a queen on the bed. Alok was delighted, and he took off his shirt too. He jumped on the bed and began kissing and caressing her. Two minutes later, a bundle of fifty-rupee notes flashed on Reshma's right side. A stunned Alok wondered who might be there. Much before he could think, another bundle was thrown on her left side. She violently shoved him off the bed, picked the two packets, wore her top, and left the premises.

Alok clearly recollected the man as a frequent customer at his mobile unit. Why would this high-society man pay ten thousand rupees to a hooker and trap him? He got the answers from Rudra in a series of unrelenting blows and hard punches. He tried to defend himself. He could scream all he wanted, but he knew nobody would hear him, or come to his rescue.

"Who is your boss? Tell me," Rudra hit him hard on the face.

"Jaani. He is Jaani," Alok was left with no alternative.

"Who devised the plan to kill Sagar?" Rudra hit him again.

"No, I don't know. I really don't know. Please stop beating me," Alok was sincere. However, his truth was not acceptable. Rudra tormented him for over forty minutes. He described where they lived. It was a shitty place in Wadarbandyapalya, and there were several like him. His tormentor was interested in Sagar's killers, of whom he had absolutely no idea. He could not give him any leads as to who made the threatening call to Rudra. That he was a very ordinary foot soldier in the lousy world was not accepted by Rudra.

Alok was gagged and his hands and legs were tied.

The final preparations for the VC pitch were closed a week in advance, and that naturally called for a celebration. Rathishree was understandably sky-high in terms of the fulfilment levels. Her heart went beyond the skies. She resigned her full-time job at Accenture. The emails, the advertisements on social media, with whatever the limited budget, the traction of traffic from www.pp.com and their own videos on the social media platforms were comprehensively analyzed again by Rathi before sending the final pitch to the VCs. She was sure that Sagar would not have done it any differently.

Rathi asked Rudra to compile the breakfast order list on the LOVE 130504 group. She was particular that the neighbouring couple must make it, and the holiday made it easier for them. Within their little group, she requested to make it a vegetarian-only order after Veena accepted the invitation. Koyal was not sure of the largesse, but she did not mind it much. The exclusive concession impressed a certain somebody who let out a low whistle on the first meeting.

'Masala Dosa Meeting' made for a proper heading even as idli, vada and poha were also specially ordered. Josh, Veena, Yashu, Rudra, Koyal, Jim and Rathi sat in a circle around the table. The seven took breakfast, and Rathi set the ball rolling.

"The pitch has been shot across to the Real-Time Sync VC, and we have managed to send it a week in advance. A toast to the pitching," Rathi raised her hand.

"Hip, hip, hurray! Hip, hip, hurray!" The team was vocal in the support. Josh and Rudra too joined in the approval.

"Now, I will sound very formal, and yet this needs to be recorded. How did we manage to send a presentation and detailed pitching a week in advance when in our own assessment, we might have been delayed by at least two weeks? That advancement has been possible because of the one and only Veena Rao. One round of applause to her, please," Rathi asked her team. The cheers in this round were louder than the earlier one. It was fair because the first one was for themselves, and what Veena did was support without expectations of any rewards.

"Rathishree, our thanks should not be in mere words. We must give our regards in terms of Esops. I say this especially in light of the grave challenging issues solved for us by Veena," Yashu chimed in seriously.

"I agree," Jim approved.

"Amen," Koyal.

"Thank you, Veena," Rudra was grateful too.

"Come on, Yashu and Rathi. You are flattering me. Rathi walked me through the presentation, and explained to me the overall journey. Sagar's vision and work, and your effort as a team is the sole reason for your success. If you need to thank somebody beyond your flat, it has to be pp.com," Veena did not give much credit to her contribution.

"Do you mean that stupid fans forum website?" Josh laughed.

"I am serious," Veena was positive about the role of pp.com in the revival of PaPi.

"My girl is very humble. I will take some credit too because I am not as humble as her," Josh joked, kissing Veena on the cheeks.

"My mistake, Josh. We are also thankful, if not grateful, to you. You have indeed spent countless hours encouraging our endeavours," Rathi raised a round of deserving applause for Josh.

"I wish your enterprise all the success," Veena took out a box of Ferrero Rocher chocolates.

"So sweet of you, Veena," Rathi thanked her friend.

"How sure are we of the pitch sailing to the coast?" asked Rudra.

"It is Sagar's path, and you are just following it. I am sure you will get the funding," Veena was positive on the glory of the enterprise.

"Seriously Veena! We want to know how you are so sharp in the software engineering front despite working on AI/ML for several years." Yashu wanted to know the secrets.

"I guess I had never forgotten my engineering chops. True, I work on completely different subjects now, AI/ML, Stat, and Math. Python and R are my day-to-day platforms. Basics always remain there. Besides, I will be brutally honest here. Your entire construction sucks, and the engineering design is fundamentally flawed. I am not saying anything new which I have not told Rathi earlier. Now, Jim's and Koyal's cases are different, and they have moved away from the engineering domain. While Rathi has been trying hard, she needs to really improve a lot if she genuinely aspires to be a real engineer. You, Yashu, on the other hand, totally suck. I have not worked with you, Rudra, so no news is good news for you. Again, sorry," Veena gave her blunt comments. She did not deconstruct the PaPi team's efforts; she demystified it.

"You rock, girl," Yashu agreed and kissed Veena on the cheek. The kiss was wetter than it should have been, and that might be because of the water the kisser had sipped.

"Even then Veena, we are keen on Esops for you. Josh, you too," Rathi insisted.

"No. I am really sorry to repeat it. First and foremost, all of my help is nothing beyond what is available on the web search. Second, it will be a conflict of interest if I accept the shares. We are friends, and it is for the friendship," Veena did not think much of her cooperation. The breakfast came to a close, and the coffee was served by Koyal.

"Come on, Veena. Stop overacting," Josh ridiculed his girl. His tone was a bit furious.

"I am not. Rules mean something, and integrity means a lot to me. I won't compromise in my contractual obligations to AT&B Finance. If my help to PaPi violates the agreement, I will certainly not help our friends. It does not matter how close we all are," Veena said aggravatedly. She did not like to explain and reiterate the same stuff over and over, especially to Josh. The coffee was a welcome reprieve from the heated argument.

"Do you have to really contradict me, Veena? For god's sake," Josh was now shouting and breathing down her neck. She turned in Rathishree's direction, smiled, and took another sip. He could not believe she was blatantly ignoring him. As she returned the coffee tumbler to the table, Josh grabbed her jaw in a tight first and turned her in his direction, "Stop the pretension. You can't ignore me. Do you understand?" She stared in his eyes without blinking.

The hosts were not sure how to stop the fight. Not only was Veena the senior-most among them, but they also were not clear on how to pacify Josh. Besides, it was their personal matter, and even Veena was not backing down from the confrontation. Koyal hinted at Jim to take Josh out for a smoke break. Veena's jaws were still in Josh's fist and her eyes were welling up with tears. The wincing could not be more apparent.

"A smoke break, Josh," Jim intervened. It was only after hearing the words that Josh released the girl in pain. Much before he could pull the chair out, Veena stormed out in tears. She did not want to really cry, but Josh's attack was vicious. The men and Yashu hit the balcony for their cigarettes, leaving Rathi and Koyal in the main hall.

"I can't forgive myself for Veena's tears. Josh is a prick for sure," Rathi was furious, "I blame myself for the mess."

"Don't be hard on yourself. The boy was crass for sure," Koyal was angry too.

"Did you see the mark on Veena's cheeks? Is he a monster or what? She cried, and I saw the tears," Rathi could not believe what had just happened.

"I saw them too. We ought to keep our guard on if it gets violent in the adjacent flat," Koyal proposed and Rathi agreed.

Yashashwini was walking away from the exit gate of Greenville when a biker on Royal Enfield Classic 350 trailed her and called out her name. She turned around to find Josh Khandelwal.

"Hi, Josh. I did not expect you at all," the charming lady smiled her best.

"Hop along," Josh invited.

"Oh, no. I am waiting for an Ola cab. It is on the way and will reach the corner in five minutes. Going to Koramangala for some work. Thank you." Yashu grinned.

"Hey, look. I have an off day today. Veena's too bloody busy at her work, and I am bored like hell. I have the full day to kill. Let me drive you to your destination then," Josh wanted her company.

"Veena might not like it. Besides, my cab is on the way. I don't have the mandatory helmet either. Sorry, Josh," Yashu started to walk towards the pick-up point.

"Here," Josh flashed the extra helmet he was carrying, "if it is still too much trouble for the lady, I don't mind paying the Ola cancellation fees." He winked, and she could not refuse him any further. She wore the helmet and sat on the rear seat.

The bike strode leisurely even on the empty patches of the road. Yashu was surprised over the approach. He explained the drive on massive beasts of the motorcycle is enjoyed in slow driving and the machine was not a sports bike to be ripped on the asphalt. Yashu again expressed reservation over Veena's likely objections, and he insisted they were all grown-ups. Besides, it was never that the scholar lady was not given the first choice.

"Oh, I am a second choice for you then," Yashu groaned.

"The same as I am a second option for you," Josh told her. After all, Rudra was her first choice. "Do you mind sipping beer at Gilly's Resto Bar?" he offered.

"Sure," Yashu was always game for drinks. The two then changed the destination. As they were about to draw suite in Gilly's Resto, Josh excused himself for a quick smoke, and Yashu asked for one too.

"You look stressed. Trouble in paradise?" she expressed herself freely.

"No, I am not. That's my fucking official response, and I am here to beat the shit out of the official status quo," Josh was desperate.

"Office issues?" she asked, and he vociferously nodded. "Oh. That's depressing. Veena?"

"Yeah! You invest two fucking crores on a flat, and this lady has work of more than twenty-four hours during our mutual ten hours," he crushed the butt in the large ashtray. "Let's order some chilled beers." They went inside and he placed the order.

"Did you give it a thought that she might be really busy with her office? Rathishree was telling me how laser-sharp Veena is in software engineering, and that too despite not working in the domain for several years. If a genius requires more time, that must be some helluva work, isn't it?" Yashu tried to see the other side.

"You know it better, is it? Tell me Yashu, do you or your flatmate Rathishree know Veena better than me? Now, imagine the roles reversed. Do you think I can't pick up extra work in my current role of assistant manager at KR Global Hotels? Or that I can't engage myself in app development? What will you and Rathishree call me then? Tell me, truthfully," Josh made a clear case.

"Oh, we will without a second thought accuse you of either an affair at the office or that you are losing interest in Veena," Yashu confessed freely.

"If you don't mind, please come over here, I need to show you something," Josh had a fascinating video clip.

Josh showed her the debut of a brand-new couple resort in Goa that was tantalizingly named as MayaBeacha. It was an entirely different kind of resort, and its name itself was pretty intriguing.

Responding to the Lakshagriha conspiracy of the demon Duryodhan, the Pandavas at a later stage set up a mesmerizing palace with the help of another demon named Mayasura. The castle of illusions lured Duryodhan into a humiliating experience. Maya means dreams, and *beacha* is the reference to a beach, and this resort of fantasy for a couple was constructed at the Ashvem beach. The MayaBeacha was an AI/ML automated I-I stay at Goa, with I-I meaning isolated-on-island. The resort was a tunnelled accommodation that ran a few hundred metres in the sea. The rocks on the two sides of the bending meant the tunnel did not block the public access to the beach in any manner. Thousands of cameras imposed the live impressions on the tunnel's inner digital screen giving the real beach experience. The hologram technology imposed three-dimensional images from the beach scenario inside the tube and offered the practical experience of a beach. The difference being that you would be incognito, and the beach inside the tunnel would be entirely yours. Besides, MayaBeacha is complete with a robotic servant who takes care of the requirements without a thing to worry about.

"Now, I might appear a lesser professional than all of you among the occupants of the two flats. But I am the one and only employee cum manager of MayaBeacha – a job that I do on a part-time basis. The room tariff for this couple resort is one lakh rupees per day. I took Veena there for three days amid the heavy expenditures of resurrecting VJ. And what does the great scholar do on the first day of occupying the flat? 'Not Available' board! I must be a fool, isn't it?" Josh was annoyed with his girlfriend. His impassioned outburst to Yashu fetched an entirely unexpected response from her. She was totally engrossed in the video.

After the third view of the video, Yashu could not hide her desire of being in the little paradise. "Can you somehow manage a two-day stay for me at MayaBeacha? Please," she begged him.

"That's just a little favour. Work out the schedule with Rudra and tell me the dates," Josh knew where this was headed.

"I am sure Rudra can't afford this luxury. For me, please," Yashu bit her lower lip.

"Two lakh rupees is too much of a manipulation. You know it, Yashu," he teased her, bringing his lips deadly close to hers. The dim light of the resto bar helped them get cosy.

She sealed the deal with a kiss. The damsel returned home in an Ola cab.

Dinner had the usual mix of preferred food on the table of the entrepreneurs. In a very casual enquiry, the engagement date of Jim-Koyal was revealed. The box of sweets from Bijnor was the testimony of the commitment from their parents. Rudra and Yashu exchanged glances, furthering their commitment.

"Rathishree, you too need to move on. We are sure Sagar will bless your decision from the skies," Jim encouraged her.

"I am married to PaPi," Rathi was indeed dedicated.

"Loyalty means jack. Sagar said so, lest we forget," Rudra reminded the principles of their mentor.

"Ah, and then he insisted on the context, my dear flatmate," Rathi had not forgotten a thing about her love. "Can we move to another topic all the same, please?"

It was time for dessert, and the email alert from the mobile stopped Rathi from taking a spoonful of her icecream. She unlocked the mobile, and there was the anticipated email from Real-Time Sync VC. Her heart stopped beating until she opened the communication entirely, and the first word after the salutation was "Congratulations!" She continued reading the email further, and apart from the regular text verbatim on the board approving the pitching, the amount approved was two million dollars for PaPi!

Rathi gobbled up her icecream, bewildering her flatmates, and then she flung the mobile on the table and punched her fist in the air a dozen times. Koyal read the email. The dream was finally coming true. They had pulled it off. The celebration cries filled the flat, and there were smiles and laughter all around. Against all her protests, Jim and Rudra carried Rathi on their shoulders and paraded three rounds around the dining table. A full hour later, after calling their friends and the Bansals in Vidisha, the five dumped themselves on the couch in ecstasy.

Yashu then reminded everyone to invite their neighbours.

"Sure, drop in the invite in the group LOVE 130504," Rathi gave the nod.

"Veena exited the group. Will you call her personally? You are closest to her among us. After all, her help is unquestionably very significant in our progress," Koyal asked the head honcho. Yashu was keying in the group.

"Yashu, hold it for a while. I am not sure, and it is deplorable. Not only has Veena exited the group, but she had also refused to meet me and declined all my invites to come over here. I did not want to go over to their flat without an invitation. When I caught her walking from the lift to her door, it was even more of a sorry affair. The dark circles around her eyes and pale face stopped me from greeting her. Yes, Josh drops in here every day, and at most, we can invite him. It is for the couple to resolve their issues. I feel terribly sorry," Rathi was in an awful position.

"We will then not invite Josh explicitly. When he is here, we will appraise him and ask him to get Veena. Fair?" Jim proposed, and it was accepted by the five.

A lot more other happy discussions onwards, Rudra raised a critical issue.

"The threat is always lingering on our heads. We can't remain idle," Rudra opened the Pandora 's Box.

"We have not been idle. The press conference and other actions later, we have reported the threat call to the police too. We need to have faith in the system," Rathi elaborated the proactive actions taken by them.

"I am scared, Rathishree, not for me alone. I might have received the call, but the target does not stop with me. Now that you are leading the PaPi operations from the front, I am scared for you too. The mafia is certainly on the loose," Rudra reiterated his stance.

"Rudra and Jim, Koyal and Yashu, the mafia threat was my foremost concern when Sagar and Rudra were toying with the idea of Mobile*puri*. I am not saying I had warned you right from the beginning. But today is what it is, and there is no wishing it away. Sagar lost his life by brushing off the threat. We were fools to continue with PaPi. There is only one way to get out of this mess, and that is to abandon PaPi entirely. It also means we have to show the middle finger to his memories. Don't presume that even if we pull off the VC funding, and sell off our stakes at whatever stages, we will become free of this threat. You want to touch that money, Sagar's memory or otherwise, you kiss the threat. That fortune and the associated risk are inseparable. For me, Sagar's memory is entangled between the two. You want safety, you have to kiss the fortune good-bye. It is clear to me. The choice is yours to make," Rathi had measured the risk all the while.

"Rathishree, I fully understand your emotions. But we have to hit back at the mafia. There is no other way," Rudra insisted. Rathi was now startled by the remark.

"What does hitting back even mean? Please clarify, what's on your mind?" Rathi was still in disbelief. She did not like the direction of the conversation.

"You got me right, Rathishree. We hit back," Rudra looked into her eyes. Everybody was silent.

"No," Rathi said after two minutes of stoic silence. "We are engineers and professionals. We will never be criminals. *Never. Ever. Be. Criminals.* We all keep out of these stupid ideas." She stood up and went to her bedroom. She had enough confidence in Rudra that he wouldn't be doing anything stupid. Koyal and Jim went to their bedroom while Rudra and Yashu went to the balcony for cigarettes.

Jaani was now getting restless living under the lockdown. He was bored with playing the same game of cards, Rummy to be precise, with Baja. He often regretted declining Tiku's multiple offers of getting rid of Baja. However cruel Baja might be, but he was the most benevolent of them. Nothing, in Jaani's assessment, compensated for the traitor smell that reeked from Tiku's body. Turning over Baja would have eternally meant a bloody price to be paid. After all, the crime world was underground for a reason. This smaller network was unassumingly smaller. Getting rid of Baja was the same as foregoing his sister's family in the native state. He was nothing without his elder sister's support, and she meant the world to him. The shadow truths could not be hidden from self, and he knew the respect and friendship with Baja was a mutual relationship. Baja was definitely predictable and boring. But he did the same set of moves with a lot of grace. Besides, Baja could produce hookers out of thin air, an art he could never master.

The sun could not shine better at 11 a.m., and he went out for a little stroll to the nearby paan shop. Inspector Limbekai had issued a strict warning that the two should not be seen in the core areas of Bengaluru. Baja asked if the two could hide in smaller hustlings of Thirumalapura, 8th Mile, Tumkuru Road, and the location was okayed. The sixty plus Jaani was almost worn out from the little crimes. He was glad that he never got into narcotics and political crimes. It was his practice to finish two beedis while the paan shop owner packed ten betel leaves stuffed with tobacco.

With the polythene bag securely containing the ten paans, two packs of beedi and a Scissor's pack of ten, he lit the third beedi and began walking home. He received a call on his mobile and as he received it with a hello, Jaani bumped into someone and the mobile fell from his hands. The lady fell down on the road, and she cursed him in Kannada. Annoyingly, he said, "*gaali kyun deti ho, beti.*" The woman struck her forehead and replied in Hindi that it was not her fault if her expressing being hurt in her native language was interpreted as a curse by him. Jaani profusely apologized and picked her mobile, and begging forgiveness, went home.

Two hours later, Jaani's mobile rang again. He received the call, and it was the voice of a lady. She told him from the other end that their mobiles were swapped, and he was speaking with her mobile, and she was using his.

"One minute," Jaani knew that he had to be cautious, and recollected the event. Ah, it was he who had picked up her phone and handed it over. It further meant that the confusion was genuine and that the lady was no spy of the police or a rival gang.

"Okay, come to the paan shop," he agreed to swap the mobiles again.

The mobile had not been tampered with, and no calls were made either. Satisfied, he returned home. The lady walked two hundred metres west and handed the mobile to a biker sitting on an RX-100. Did the biker mark Jaani and Baja?

Rudra was getting totally frustrated with the captive Alok. Every hour of captivity increased the risk, and he was not able to extract more useful information from the vendor boy. Apart from Jaani's name, there was no juice in the revelations. Alok confessed to having never seen the face of the mafia leader. His other source confirmed the presence of two vendor boys named Bholu and Ghumroo in the shanties of Wadarbandyapalya. Could he take those two under captivity? No, that was not possible as their selling points were at South End Circle, Jayanagar and Bapuji Nagar bus stand. Besides, he was not running a police department to take as many suspects as it fancied him. Shikhan was long dead, and Barfi fled without any trace. Jarokh was missing since Sagar's demise. None of this information meant anything in making a headway.

"Go berserk," advised the ego. Rudra entered the small studio apartment on the Greenville terrace. Without any second thought, he started unleashing vicious blows and kicks on the kidnapped guy. "Tell me, you bastard, who threatened me. Speak up, you cunt. Tell me, you whore," Rudra kicked him two more times. His mobile started ringing, and he answered it.

"Did the parrot sing the song?" asked the caller.

"Not yet," Rudra answered.

"Time to pack him off to a secluded place. Don't risk any further," the caller switched to Plan B.

"Fine," Rudra said and looked at his victim. The man stared at him. The audacity! The blood rushed. He felt like kicking the rogue again, and as the shoe was about to hit Alok, he realized that the eyes were not staring at him. The eyes were out of the socket.

"Hello, hello," the voice felt the signal was lost. "There? Rudra, there?"

"Yes, the parrot is no more," Rudra whimpered.

"Look, listen, listen…" and more instructions followed.

Two days and three hundred metres away near Madhuloka, Alok's mutilated body was found in a gunny bag. In the absence of Baja and Jaani, Tiku Singh took ownership of Alok's dead body through other vendor boys. The post-mortem report attributed a left-hander as the attacker. The sniffer dogs were not useful as it had rained the previous night heavily.

8 Imli Pani Turns Sour

The admin of www.pp.com shot a message to the user ID PPWila, aka, Viraj Jain. The short message simply read "An update for you. Come Online." Viraj was happy to know that the admin tried his best to help him. "Coming at 6:30. I have an update of my own," Viraj replied. He was indeed happy that his worries were coming to an end soon.

Was it time for him to get settled down in life? Was marriage on the cards? Or was it a promotion in the new company? He was not much worried about marriage or development, as the two are a matter of eventuality. He provided a bullshit reason over the gap in his resume. He had a difficult time obtaining the relieving letter from his previous company. He was marked as an absconder, and that would have made it horribly difficult to get a decent job. Viraj showed up to the HR and explained the exceptional circumstances when he was lost as in a time warp. Earlier, he had met the manager. He had excellent relations during his working period. Viraj said he was not looking to be rehired or a positive letter of recommendation. He simply begged not to be mentioned absconding in the relieving letter.

The HR mellowed after the support of the manager, and it helped Viraj to secure a job in Gurugram.

"What's your update, Viraj?" asked the admin.

"Sure, PP. My parents and family are finally free from the clutches of the mafia. Thank god, and you too," Viraj could not discuss the matter with anybody else.

"Oh, that's really very good news. How did it happen? You are free not to disclose. But I am happy for you," the admin replied.

"Oh, not a problem at all. I can tell you for sure. We were asked for a ransom of ten lakh rupees by Tiku Singh's men. In fact, I spoke with Tiku, and he was willing to let go of us for that ransom, and we were certainly happy to get rid of the monster. You might say we were wrong, but there are difficult choices to make in life. Thanks a lot for your support," Viraj was grateful.

"Happy for you, Viraj," the admin granted the choice was indeed tricky.

"What was your update?" asked Viraj.

"Does the mafia world matter now? I think you shouldn't worry any further," the admin hypothesized, and the engineer agreed.

Rathishree got busy with the release of the first part of the half-a-million dollars investment. A significant criticism of the investors was the name of the enterprise, and now it was impossible to rebrand PaPi. Rudra was more drowned in alcohol these days, and he cut a very sorry figure when he presented himself during the meetings and deliberations. Another idea of Rathi's approved by the investor was to create a documentary film on the style and enigma of Sagar Bansal. The budget was cut down by a third, much to Rathi's chagrin. It was down to five lakh rupees, but then Rathi did not complain. The documentary film was more important than the magnitude of the budget because the idea was to light up the memory. She understood that Sagar was no superstar. For them, yes. To the investors, a firm no.

Yashu found Rathi's regime too professional. For instance, it was now not optional to resign from the parent company, and the bigger problem was that beyond the Esops benefit, the salaries were not increased by more than thirty per cent. Rudra was too tense these days to show up and protest. The biggest loser in the shift was Yashu because the investors rejected any salary higher than Rathi's among the founding members. The only way for Yashu to get a higher wage was to clear the interview process and join as an outsider and forego the Esops. It was a colossal damper for Yashu, and she cribbed that if Sagar was around, she would have got her due. Furiously, she hit the balcony for a cigarette.

"How long do you think she will be furious?" Koyal asked.

"Who cares! The VCs are no jokers, and I really like it that way. We can't run away with all their investments as our next month's salary. I am not sure about Sagar, but I can't tolerate the alcoholic Rudra. But I guess it is not a personal choice. I really hope he rebounds," Rathi was sure that the investors were tracking their performance too.

"Do you think Rudra will resign from Accenture?" Jim asked.

"I don't think Yashu will allow that. She has already asked me if it is possible to transfer Rudra's share to her. That has only one direction. It is not just that, she wanted Sagar's shares to be divided equally among the five of us. You can only guess her shock when I said it is all going to the Bansal family," Rathi was clear about the way the investments were going.

"Does the Bansal family want to exercise Sagar's voting powers too?" Jim wanted to know if Rathi could share those details too.

"The investor's Real-Time Sync VC has been observing PaPi for much longer than we would like to believe. While they were pleased that we wanted to give the Esops to the Bansal family, the important condition was that there would be no voting power ever for them. For instance, they can decide to sell the shares, but they can't decide a damn thing until Real-Time Sync VC is the majority stakeholder. Yashu takes things very lightly, and she is almost back to the dark days. I had to convince the board a lot to retain her," Rathi revealed.

"Can Rudra transfer his shares to Yashu?" Koyal asked.

"Did you read the documents carefully? It is a take-it-leave-it offer. If Rudra places the special request, they will ask him to fuck off," Rathi giggled.

"And our neighbours' case?" Jim was curious.

"It will be a double fuck-off case, for us," Rathi was sad the moment Veena's reference turned up. Yashu finished her cigarette and returned to the hall.

"Fine! Rudra was blabbering that he might have to exit PaPi if his shares are not transferred to me," Yashu began on an impossible note.

"Yashu! This may look crazy to you, but here is the naked truth. Sagar had kicked off the investment discussions with Real-Time Sync VC, and, please pay more attention all of you, our proposal was rejected by every other investor. So, apart from the current VC, we have no alternative. Next, there is no such thing as 'If Sagar was there…' logic, because, and as much as I still love Sagar, the VC gives zero fucks about him. Their terms and conditions are utterly non-negotiable, and they will not entertain smaller fish like us. To cut a long story short, Rudra has to join the VC invested PaPi first for any consideration of his shares. Now, if you allow Yashu, we need to discuss hiring and new office space," Rathi wanted to move to other problems.

"Just one minute, Rathi. Flexibility was our greatest strength, and I am bored with the programming by now. I would like to move over to the PaPi social media tasks. Jim can move over to the software maintenance," Yashu was creating obstacle after obstacle.

"A rejig?" Rathi wondered.

"You might call it a rejig, and I would like to call it flexibility. You were flexible at the beginning and donned so many hats. I want a different one now," Yashu continued to persist with her demands.

"You and I cannot make a unilateral decision. Jim, what is your take?" Rathi asked.

"No thanks. I am fine with my role," Jim simply did not know why they were discussing the out-of-the-list topic to such great lengths.

"I guess he can't have his demand of sticking to the current role as that would be a unilateral decision too. So Rathi, you are fine with me moving to Jim's role, and that makes it a democratic and majority rule. Thanks Jim," Yashu was walking away with her demand.

"God, Yashu! What's wrong with you? Amid an overhaul of the company when we are busy with a long list of unending tasks of errands – hiring, staffing, training, finding a new office, developing new software, deciding marketing strategy, multi-media strategy, operations, scaling, developing other necessary verticals, and so on... Where is the time for transitions to the new roles? Where is the necessity? And what happens if one of us does not fit into the new role? It will be chaos all over. Now, please don't drive me crazy. We move to other points awaiting discussion," Jim thundered.

"I agree with Jim," Rathi could not waste any more thoughts on the rejig.

"Not so fast, Jim. Look, I know I will shine in my new role. I can't take responsibility for your failures. I can merely give you the transition. Rathi, we need to have a serious relook at the roles," Yashu was adamant. Koyal was so turned off that she felt it better to focus on the work at hand.

"Fine Yashu, tell me point-blank. Are you determined to screw the overall progress? Now, let me tell you as a senior. Real-Time Sync VC might not have technical genius like Veena Rao, but they sure have management genius. As Veena roasted the platform created by us and chided us as rank amateurs, are you now determined to give a stick to those management tycoons to beat the shit out of us? Because if you are determined on the new role, it will be the end of us. We can pack our bags right now. And let me clarify Yashu, I will have no regrets of shutting down PaPi more than the disappointment of not being able to meet your little demand. Do you want a change of roles?" Rathi clarified the consequences.

"Oh, I am sorry team, I did not think this deep. I am really sorry, and I mean it," Yashu said and went for a smoke yet again.

"Why is she such a fool?" Koyal now opened up.

"God knows! Might be Rudra, or might be the hormones," Rathi was less amused.

"Oh! You did not get it, Rathi?" wondered Jim.

"Are you serious?" Rathi was certainly not sure of the reason for Yashu's demand.

"Ha, ha. The budget of nearly five lakhs for the documentary on Sagar would have allowed her to make some quick money," Jim guessed it correctly. The impatient spinster did not realize the difference between long-term and short-term plans. She always thought of instantaneous gains. A foolish strategy because what happens in an instant is not a term, and if it is not a term, there is no plan but only action.

"*Baja bhai*! *Buri khabar*," Jaani hated to wake up his boss of two decades to break the bad news to him at six in the morning. Baja woke up violently and shook his head vicariously.

"Baja bhai, it's me. I hate to break the bad news to you. Tiku Singh was killed two hours ago. Ghumroo and Dhyan have been killed along with him," Jaani relayed the news.

"Who killed them?" Baja asked.

"We don't know anything," Jaani said truthfully.

"Move," and the old partners in crime vacated the premises under two minutes. They knew that they had to get to the politician Kshitij Singh's home. The politician was head of the Samrudya Party. There was no other recourse.

Baja took out his mobile and dialled the one-time dial mobile number of Dr Sripad Limbekai. He was lucky that the call went through. In their limited capability, the total bribe paid over the past decade was a little over ten crore rupees.

"Hello!" the inspector answered the call.

"Are we next?" asked Baja.

"No. Hello, hello," the inspector gave the impression of not being able to hear the question clearly.

"Thank you," and Baja put an end to the call. He next addressed his pal of many decades, "*apna number nahi hai*." They were not on the hit list.

An hour later, they were relaxing in the outhouse of Kshitij Singh.

The details of the deaths of Tiku Singh, Ghumroo and Dhyan started pouring in. The cuts on their bodies were similar to the scars on Alok's body, and the attack on the trio happened four hundred metres away from Tiku's hiding location.

"*Badla to hoga! Magar khoon ki holi se nahi*," the politician assured his henchmen. The assurance was that there would be bloodless vengeance. Baja agreed without any alternative while Jaani swallowed the bitter pill. It was not about Tiku, it was about them.

Rudra was totally desolate since the killing of Alok. He had managed to escape the police until now, but he was not sure how long he would be able to stretch his luck. His mobile rang. It was no consolation that it was not a private number, because the call came from the hooker Reshma. She knew his dirty little secret. A single call from her to the police that she seduced Alok to the terrace of Greenville and took ten thousand rupees to trap the poor vendor boy, and he would be locked away for good. He received the call, and as expected, she was waiting for him at the studio apartment.

Why was he always shivering these days? What a fool he was! What if she was a hooker? In her early thirties, she was not an out of shape whore. All he had to do once in a week was to carry one or two thousand rupees and a little pack of condoms. That's it, and he resolved to overcome his fears forever. He had already paid her twenty thousand rupees until now, inclusive of the ten thousand rupees for luring Alok. Why couldn't Rudra keep a mistress like the biggies? He marvelled at his ability to convert the threat into another opportunity.

Unlike the last three times, Rudra went with confidence and conviction to the studio apartment. He opened the door, and Reshma was lying on the bed with a smirk on her face. She was confident he must have brought the five thousand rupees. Why did he latch the door?

"No smartness, Mr Rudra. Keep your money on the table and get going," she warned him.

"I have extra money, Reshma darling," Rudra turned next to her bedside.

"I will call the police," she reminded him of the consequence. Reshma confidently stood up and looked him in the face.

"Call them! We will both go to jail. Do you want me to fuck you here, or in the jail?" Rudra laughed. He did not give her much time to think and kissed her full on the lips. Overpowering her, he undressed her in under two minutes and then using the condom, dominated and banged her for two hours. He made it a point to slap her hard on the cheeks, face cheeks as well as the ass cheeks. When he was done with her, he laid an extra thousand rupees for the pleasure. Reshma realized her folly. She could no longer threaten to send him to jail without being prepared to go to jail herself. The extra thousand rupees would not be there the next week, and after a month or two, he would not give her more than a thousand rupees per week. Third month onwards, he would also visit her at least twice a week. Every single time, he would be rough with her. She laughed after realizing that Rudra knew who she was. A whore.

Rathishree regretted driving Veena to tears. She could not undo that one wrongdoing to the most innocent and selfless person she had met in a long while. Rathi tried to sneak in when Josh's mother was visiting the VJ flat, or when Veena's heart patient mother Shyamala Rao and father Pratik Rao visited the neighbour. Veena proved too hard a problem to solve, and beyond the smile and a simple greeting, Veena refused to speak another word. Veena's boyfriend Josh found a better companion in Rudra, and the two would be either drinking at home or at a venue where drinks were served cheap and fast.

Yashu being Yashu flooded a thousand rumours regarding Veena and Josh. In one story, Josh was useless, while Veena was infertile in another. Sometimes both were useless. There were further conflicting reports over flat ownership. While Josh insisted that he had paid for the flat with inherited money, Romila Tagore emphasised that apart from the initial inscription on the name etched in the marble stone, Josh was not fit enough to be even a sweeper in the exquisite apartment. What was confirmed for sure was that VJ was the youngest pair to own a flat in Greenville in their own name. The dual apartment had parking space for four cars and at least six bikes. This was not surprising. However, unique to the VJ style of getting things done, the owners had closed the parking garage. Rudra, Jim and Yashu tried to find out but they could not confirm which cars and bikes were parked inside the closed parking space. Yamaha MT-09 and the iconic RD 350 were rumoured to be two special bikes, and at least two swanky cars were securely parked there for sure.

Yashu tried her best at flirting with Josh, and even then, she could not get out a single piece of information about the parking. It was weirder that Josh's own bike, Classic 350, was always parked in the shared bike zone. On being asked why he would not park in the dedicated space, he simply claimed that he was too lazy to carry the individual swipe cards for the secure parking. When Josh, Rudra and Yashu were drowned in beer, Josh had talked about the MT-09 and RD 350 in the passing. When Rudra asked why he didn't take out those monsters, Josh replied that Veena drove them. Yashu insisted Josh had said nothing like that, and Rudra said he felt it was told. Josh, of course, never entertained any further questions over the secure parking.

Rathi was thinking so much about Veena that she ridiculed herself over her vague thoughts. Without any expectation, Rathi shot a message to Veena over chat if she could join her for Koyal's engagement with Jim the next day at the famous Indira Nagar Club. "I will try," was the first encouraging reply from the adorable genius in what seemed like centuries. Veena further laid the condition that if she could make it, they would be chauffeured in a car of the scientist's choice. If she failed, Rathi was to have her back up plan. "Agreed," Rathi confirmed without any hesitation.

When Veena said she would try to make it to the engagement, Rathi was positive that a sincere attempt would undoubtedly be made. Clad in a heavy plated golden embroidered half pink saree for the occasion, Rathi was ready. She had twenty minutes before Veena would confirm one way or another. Rudra and Yashu had left earlier in the day for an early morning breakfast at Vidyarthi Bhavan. Josh did not have leaves left at his KR Global Hotels workplace. Rathi was busy attending the emails when an alert beeped on her MobileChat. She opened the chat app, and it was a message from Veena that she would be ready in five minutes for the event. A very positive development. Rathi had been longing to meet the vivacious diva. "A scholar, what's wrong with you, Rathi," she corrected herself.

When Veena turned up at the elevator, Rathi totally adored the smart casual, neck top, brown sleeveless top, and the dark blackish-brown skirt-wearing lascivious Veena in a five-inches heel. As the duo entered the parking zone, Rathi was stunned that except for the black lipstick, Veena had absolutely zero makeup. She was not sure if Jim would go ahead with the engagement if his eyes fell on this smoking hot pie. "Again, what's wrong with you, Rathi," she double corrected the beyond uncontrollable thoughts beating in her heart. However, Rathi knew the source of the problem, and it was primarily Koyal and Yashu who were admirers of Veena's bootyliciousness. The ever sombre Koyal also remarked that if she were ever to turn into a lesbian, it would be for the stunning neighbour. "What's wrong with you, and why can't you just shut up!" Rathi was angry with herself.

The Ford Endeavour turned up to pick the ladies from the Greenville portico. Veena checked about the progress of PaPi, and how the scalability was turning up. They discussed office, new furniture, hiring, interviews and even the stakeholdership. Rathi could easily see that Veena was holding a lot back on the technical inputs and instead worked around that path.

The event hall of the Indira Nagar Club was decorated like a Hindu-Christian festival. The shades of Karnataka decor took precedence over elements of Kerala and Uttar Pradesh. Rathi could make out it must have been Koyal's idea as the flatmate was head-over-heels in love with Kannada, Kannadigas and Karnataka. She could guarantee Veena was grabbing the most eye-pops. After Veena and Rathi were snapped on the stage with the now committed couple, Koyal insisted on a solo photo with Rathi, and Veena walked off the stage.

"The team let us down today. Sorry, Koyal," Rathi regretted the five could not be on the stage as Rudra and Yashu were at least an hour away from the venue.

"That's fine, and thanks for getting Veena. That is some solace," Koyal thanked the bestie.

"Are you sure you are grateful for that? Jim's eyes were searching for her among the guests more than a handful of times," Rathi teased.

"Ah! That's why they say that half information is always dangerous," Jim joined the whispering. "I was scanning for Veena, and there is no doubt about that. But where you are wrong, Rathi, is the conclusion that I was doing it for myself." He pointed his eyes in Koyal's direction, and the three laughed. The long queue compelled Rathi to go off-stage. Lunch was being served in the adjoining hall, and Rathi and Veena went towards it. Fifteen minutes later, when they were almost finishing, Veena got a call from her uncle, Fanindra Rao. Her uncle wanted to hand over Tirupati prasadam to his niece. Three minutes afterwards, Rathi and Veena hit the Endeavour car and met her uncle.

"*Yalli, aa bolimaga kanasta illa,*" Fanindra cussed Veena's lover in the slangiest words of Kannada.

"*Ena idu doddappa, kaialli prasada, matte nalige mele ketta pada,*" Veena hugged her uncle and told him that he should not keep slang words on the tongue when there was sacred prasadam in hand. Rathi then wondered if Veena was okay with her uncle abusing Josh using vulgar words.

"*Aa halka nanna magange baidre, Devaru nagatare,*" Fanindra said that cursing her man Josh would be considered as a pious act in the eyes of god.

"Nivu heladimele nijjane irate," Veena agreed with her uncle that his words were always wisdom.

The uncle took out a Dairy Milk chocolate and gave it to his niece and remarked that if he did not give a chocolate to his little doll, the visit would remain incomplete. The uncle and niece conversed for another ten minutes. How strange! Rathi could not help but register that the uncle treated the twenty-seven-year-old Veena like a girl who was not even ten years old. He did not bother to address the niece as a grown-up in the presence of her friends. She had seen a similar display earlier too. No, it was not her parents Shyamala and Pratik Rao who treated Veena similarly, but Josh's mother, Roshini Khandelwal.

How could a girl like Veena keep up with Josh's rogue ways? Rathi's evaluation and analysis were intervened by the uncle who bid them adieu.

"Dodappa jhadisi ugadru Joshge," Rathi now spoke with Veena in Kannada. Veena smiled as she had forgotten that Rathi followed every bit of her conversation with her uncle. The two women continued in their mother tongue.

"Yeah! Now that you know who my uncle is, keep it a little secret from Josh. With his sucking records in academics, he was never employment ready. More so, on the attitude front. We were madly in love, and I pulled strings with my uncle and somehow got a job for him as a deputy manager in a branch of KR Global Hotels. I was mistaken with Josh, the philanderer. My family tolerated his smoking and occasional drinking. But now, as you might have heard too, uncle found him trying to get lucky with the financially weaker spinsters at the hotel," Veena was devastated by this development.

"Are you on the verge of breaking up?" Rathi asked.

"I am very fond of his mother, and she likes me too. That is not the only problem. Roshini and my mother know each other for twenty-five years, and so I am still trying to see if it can work one or the other way with Josh. I hate to tell this to myself, but it is not working. We sleep in different bedrooms," Veena again broke down in tears. The traffic was too much, almost at a standstill. Rathi simply took Veena's head on her lap and consoled her. The emotional stress was so profound that Veena fell asleep.

"*Ye Mukesh zinda hai na?*" Baja asked Jaani if Mukesh was still alive.

"*Haa,*" Jaani replied affirmatively.

"We had set up the network of three hundred seller boys. The empire was not built in a day. These bloody engineers want to sell the stupid tika puri online and mint money. Can't they apply engineering things for refined problems? Monkey shit! One after another, over a hundred boys are missing. Are we going to slaughter a hundred families in their hometown? Back in Rohtas, fifteen families came to dada and offered their heads. We can't kill everybody, can we? So, we solve our own problem," Baja was thoughtful.

"What do we do then?" Jaani was clueless.

"Get me Mukesh immediately. Alok's chest was cut open, as well as Tiku, Dhyan and Ghumroo. Isn't it?" Baja asked.

"*Samjhaa*," Jaani set about getting Mukesh to their area, and their employee turned up at the asked spot. In the tunnel, Baja left similar cuts on Mukesh as were there on the earlier murders. A little later, the masterminds set fire to the two-wheeler that brought the victim. That was the difference between Baja and Jaani. The extra gear.

Three days after the engagement came the weekend. Josh spent more evenings in the neighbours' flat than the one which he claimed to have purchased at nearly two crore rupees. His girlfriend continued in her forlorn state, keeping to their apartment. Whether Yashashwini went crazy over him, or the couple resort MayaBeacha, it made no difference to Josh. Yashashwini wanted a two-day holiday stay in the resort under all circumstances. When Jim snubbed her effort to take over the ownership of a documentary film on Sagar Bansal, she lost the opportunity to make quick bucks. Now, she was compelled to pick up whatever role was on the offer by PaPi because she was not getting a job anywhere. The kiss in the Gilly's Resto Bar was undoubtedly not enough for Josh to waive off two lakh rupees. The two knew where they were headed with all their proximity.

Yashu informed Rudra that she had to attend a distant relative's marriage in Nagpur. The relatives were close enough for her personal grace and too far away to warrant his attendance. He offered to drop her to the airport as he was feeling bored with the regular tasks, and then the master of excuses prevented him from the trouble. She boarded a taxi to the Kempegowda International Airport.

Earlier in the afternoon, Josh knocked on the office cabin of his girl in the adjoining flat.

"Yes Josh, tell me," Veena asked him.

"I need to catch the bus to Goa. Business tour, you see. I am going to check the accounts of a branch of KR Global Hotels. That means nothing to you, I am aware. On return, I have something more important to discuss. Keep your time free on Wednesday evening," Josh had a few vital matters to discuss.

"Okay," Veena did not bother to add anything more.

"What kind of a girlfriend are you…" he began bashing her again.

"Stop it, Josh! I am not listening to you. I am not used to screaming and loud voices. Please go ahead and catch your bus," Veena was shivering in fear.

"You don't stop me from completing my…" Josh was approaching her.

"Stop right there, Josh! We have quarrelled enough. One more step towards me, and I will have no recourse but to strike you," Veena had kept an armbar handy to use.

"Come on, Veena! Do you think it is enough to stop me? If force is the way, I would be between your legs right now. It does not work that way," Josh said, zeroing in on her. Trembling, she let go of the armbar. "See, you are not good at violence. Wait for me to return from Goa." He kissed her forcibly and then shoved her to the floor. At the door, he turned back and told her rudely, "You are boring, Veena. I've got better options." He left her with a wink.

Josh joined Yashashwini at the airport in the evening. The two went to the smoking-room and enjoyed the lousy taste of tobacco and lips. The flight dropped them at the airport and drawing a taxi to Ashwem beach, Josh flaunted the resort MayaBeacha. The first fully automated tunnel resort accompanied by the AI/ ML empowered sexbot Vashti welcomed the new couple. Over the next two days, Yashu and Josh had all sorts of uninhibited sex. On qualification, Vashti would be a male sexbot, and a female at other times. Fresh sea food, unlimited booze and the sea. Yashu was satisfied that if she had betrayed Rudra for these two days, the experience justified the ends. Josh wanted to have some fun as he could see she was doing some soul searching.

"Missing Rudra?" he teased her.

"As much as you are missing Veena," she laughed, and both picked their pegs.

"Ah! She is still mine," Josh grinned.

"I am not sure about you, Josh. But if I had Veena as my girlfriend, I would never betray her," Yashu was a bit serious.

"What makes you think I betrayed Veena? I already had the weekend share of sex with her earlier in the week. I am loyal to her; it is the extra loyalty that I am serving you here." Josh pulled her naked body over his and kissed her wildly. Five minutes later, after the kiss was broken, the couple laughed unabashedly.

When the Goa couple were still friends before their flight took off, Rudra packed his own little bag full of beer cans, cigarette packs and a loads of potato chips. He knew Reshma's schedule well enough. Using a different sim card, he transferred five thousand rupees to her MobileWallet. He blocked her evening time, and an hour after Yashu had left, he barged in the studio apartment knowing that Reshma would be bathing. He cunningly transferred the money back to his account from her MobileWallet.

Reshma came out of the bathroom and was shocked to see Rudra lying naked in her bed. When lust is incredibly enthralling, Rudra did not miss Yashu's love at all. She was welcome to attend a relative's out-of-station marriage every weekend. The hooker had no idea she was dealing with a monster when she began blackmailing him. It was not all in a day's work. The night was just budding, and it would be a dark night for the next sixty hours.

Josh stayed back at Goa on Monday while Yashu took an early morning flight to Bengaluru. He wanted to try other experiments at MayaBeacha. When Josh's Goan girlfriend returned from her relative's marriage at 10 a.m. at flat 1304, Rudra was sorely missing her.

"The dead body found in a tunnel earlier in the day has been identified as Mukesh's. His age was 24, and he was from Patna. Against the earlier belief that he fell in the gutter after losing control of his bike, the investigations have now revealed that Mukesh was brutally murdered. Earlier in the month, four others were found murdered in similar conditions. Tiku Singh, Alok, Dhyan and Ghumroo were all killed in the same way. Not only had these five people been murdered identically, but a common thread was also that all five of them were ordinary panipuri vendors. They had come from different parts of Uttar

Pradesh and Bihar. Is it now a crime to sell panipuri? Is it a crime to be poor? Is it a crime to come from Bihar and Uttar Pradesh? There is definitely more to these crimes than meets the eyes.

"Over the past two years, six entrepreneurs have been killed in serial accidents. Sagar Bansal, Mohit, Sripathi, Kaushik, Rodriquez, and Anjali died in road accidents. Each of them lost their lives just after the CCTV coverage range and therefore, no trace of the killers could be found. What is the connection of six entrepreneurs dying in accidents with these five murders? If those murdered were panipuri sellers, the entrepreneurs were trying to create mobile apps and platforms to sell this very same panipuri through the online channel. A sensational case hit the city after the death of Sagar Bansal. An investigation happened, and the police had arrested three panipuri sellers. But nothing further came out of those arrests.

"First, death by accident, and now death by murder. Earlier, fellow entrepreneurs made accusations of the presence of mafia in the little business of panipuri sales. Is it then possible that somebody associated with the victims of the accidents is now hitting back at the panipuri sellers? Can entrepreneurs be killers? It is too early to say anything. Hopefully, the murders will stop just like how the accidents stopped. Reporter Arya for TV 924," Arya read the news. *Was Bengaluru burning now?*

The news came as a shocker to the five on Wednesday evening. Five murders on the same lines? How was that possible? Who was killing the poor panipuri men? Rathishree heard the doorbell, and to her astonishment, it was the media from four robust TV networks. "*You can't avoid bad press*," Sagar's remark flashed in her heart, and she welcomed the press with a smile. Ten minutes later, the interview rolled on. Thankfully, drunkard Rudra was not present in the house.

"What do you have to say about the murders of poor and common panipuri sellers?" a reporter asked.

"It is really a tragedy for their families, losing their own. Sagar and I would have married a couple years down the line. It is really tough losing loved ones," Rathishree spoke with a heavy voice.

"Do you think somebody close to the deceased entrepreneur's family or friends might be behind the murders?" another reporter provoked.

"Unfortunately, we won't be able to say anything definitely or indiscriminately. We at PaPi are sure that the police will carry out its duty and nab the culprits at the earliest," Rathishree replied.

"You had sensationalized the accidents. Do you condemn the murders?" a third reporter asked.

"Definitely, we condemn the murders. Let me tell you about my trauma. Two scooters hit and ran over Sagar Bansal right before my eyes. The ambulance was not delayed. Sagar breathed his last in my lap, and we could not even take him to the hospital. We did not sensationalize the accidents at all. The other five entrepreneurs who died in similar scenarios were total strangers for us. We have nothing in common other than our passion for engineering and entrepreneurial excellence. Our motive, albeit with smaller differences among them, was always to create a better place for all of us. In the 'us' come the panipuri vendor boys, the delivery boys, the bakery where the panipuri is made, the customers, the staff working for our offices and finally us. We were not just stunned by the spate of accidents of entrepreneurs, we are disturbed by the murders of the vendors too. We are saddened by it. Finally, we also pray that the murderer, or the murderers, are nabbed at the earliest, and justice is served," Rathishree said, with steely nerves.

"Do you think the murderer is among the entrepreneurs' families and friends?" the second reporter repeated the question.

"Hi, I am Jim and a friend of Sagar Bansal. I am also a part of the PaPi enterprise. Rathishree has already answered it, but I won't mind repeating it. We have absolutely no clue about the murders. We are simple professionals, and we work passionately. We respect work, and work is also done by the poor vendors who were murdered. Please be assured that if we have any clue about the crime and/or the criminals, we will first call the police and do our duty as responsible citizens. Thank you," Jim said, very composedly.

"Do you agree the murders were gruesome?" the second reporter questioned as though his suspicions lay with the PaPi professionals.

"Of course, the murders were gruesome. As we too have seen the images on the television and the Internet, it looks like the murderer is a serial killer. Also, looking at the cuts, the murderer seems to be a left-hander," Yashashwini spoke intelligently.

The media continued for another ten minutes, and Rathishree handled the remaining questions herself. The seasoned reporters tried a lot to extract juicy and controversial statements, but were utterly disappointed. In between the questions, Rathishree asked her friends not to reply to any further questions. Ten minutes after the media left, Rathi addressed the five.

"Thank you, Jim and Yashu. Sorry, I had to stop you. I was scared they were on the verge of getting something sensational and scandalous from us. But the observation of the left-handed serial killer was remarkable," Rathi gave a thumbs up to the team.

"Rathi, how did you handle the media for thirty minutes?" Jim wondered.

"I am a politician's daughter, damn it," Rathi signed off for the night.

9 Serving the Sukha

When the dim light turned on after the members of flat 1304 returned to their room, Yashashwini could not get any sleep. Rudra had returned an hour after the media had left. She knew by experience that he would begin snoring in another two minutes.

"Rudra! Why did you murder five of them? Was Sagar's vengeance that important to you?" she asked her lover. He heard only a part of it and asked her to repeat her words.

"Are you sure you want the answers?" he asked her after she repeated her question. He could see her nodding. "Fine, Yashu. I will tell you all the truth that I know. First, will you answer a few questions of mine?" He saw her nodding again, and hence he blasted his question, "Where the hell were you over the weekend, you whore cunt?"

"What?" Yashu was startled by his question, "What's wrong with you, Rudra?"

"Listen, bitch! First answer me and come clean," Rudra gave her an opportunity.

"Stop the cussing, Rudra. Are you fine if I use similar words?" she questioned him.

"Perfect," he gave a single-word answer. Yashu stared at him in disbelief.

"What do you mean?" she got the essence and yet wanted to hear it from him.

"Fine, if it helps you that I should begin first, so be it. You know very well that I used the hooker Reshma to lure Alok into the trap. She began blackmailing me for little amounts every week. I got sick of her tactics, and on the fourth visit, I turned the tables on her. She is just thirty-two, a prostitute by profession. Now, I bang her to my heart's content and have literally made her a whore of mine.

"Now, I want you to come clean. Don't waste my time," Rudra gave her the chance to confess.

"True, I have betrayed you too. How did you guess it, though?" Yashu needed to know.

"Are you seriously dumb? The credit card that you swipe so generously, I am the recipient of those alerts," Rudra said, and he saw her face going purple.

"Well! Ever since Josh showed me the video of the serendipitous resort called MayaBeacha, I wanted to be there, one way or another. He is the sole employee and manager of the resort. It's a costly place, a lakh rupees a day. I gave in to the devil and went with him over the weekend. I am sorry, Rudra," her voice trembled at the confession.

"So, loved the resort and took a man, and not the other way round," Rudra's assessment was spot on.

"You got it," she paused, "but, but… murdering five people?" Yashu wanted an answer to that.

"Yashu, you might be intelligent, courageous and cunning. But you will wet your pants before sleeping next to a serial murderer. You know that Alok died accidentally. However, there is somebody else who is leaving the cuts on the dead bodies. Mostly, the underworld people. Trust me, if they knew it was me, I wouldn't be breathing," Rudra spilt all the truth known to him.

"What about the hooker?" Yashu had doubts because Reshma was an irrefutable witness.

"Ah! Reshma," Rudra sighed in ecstasy, "she is indeed my whore now. All she wants is to be my lifetime whore. She is also ready to stop prostitution and work as a maid here. I will stop the sexual relationship with her too. It is not a problem as big as our betrayal of one another. What have we become, Yashu, if not whores ourselves?" The two in bed decided to take the matters as they unfolded in the future on the crime front.

"Yes Rudra, we are the worst shit ourselves. I agree to stop the infidelity after a final time. Remember, you promised to get me the special one," her eyes twinkled.

"I remember," he said.

The preparations were in full swing, and the shamiyanas were set up to accommodate up to a hundred protestors. The slogan boards, the roadblocks, the effigies, chest-beating women and most importantly, the hundred mobile panipuri vendor men were all ready. "Down with Entrepreneurs," "Down with Online Sales," "Save the Panipuri Seller," and "Is it a Crime to be a Vendor?" were the slogan boards.

Effigies had 'Entrepreneur' written on the T-shirt with a dummy iPhone mobile in hand. The politician Kshitij Singh made the arrangements, and after the media-briefing, the hundred-plus vendors sat on a hunger strike at 10 a.m. Needless to say, Baja and Jaani were off the media glare. The media were asked to keep their coverage of the event on hold.

The Deputy Chief Minister had a brief meeting with the Police Commissioner. After a call to Inspector Dr Sripad Limbekai, the commissioner informed the number two minister of state that the annual bribe was to the tune of five crore rupees. The Deputy CM then called the famous politician.

"How are you Kshitij Singh?" the Deputy CM enquired, and after two minutes of cordial talking, he gave a piece of advice to Singh, "See, Kshitij brother, I understand your compulsion for the poor panipuri vendors. But you know this is not any reflection of the regional bias. What is this, Kshitij brother? For a paltry sum of five crore rupees, you are wasting everybody's time. No, no, no. There is going to be no further discussion. No means no. We can't project a poor image of the state's law and order for this minuscule issue. You need to understand that the VCs are investing billions and billions of dollars. … Listen, Kshitij bhai. If the protest is not wound up in twenty minutes, I will have to put you in jail for the murder of the vendors, and accidents of the entrepreneurs. … Good, this is what you are expected to do. … Okay, goodbye."

Kshitij was disappointed with the response, but he could understand the issue. When he came out to address the media, he did not have to take the trouble. All the journalists had long left the venue. Frustrated, he took a nearby bamboo stick and beat the crap out of one of the hapless vendors. He wanted to sternly warn Baja and Jaani that there couldn't be any more murders. One more, and he would hand them over to the police. However, their mobiles were not reachable, and after five attempts under fifteen minutes, he forgot the issue.

"The two entrepreneurs will come out of that building," was the last definitive news Baja got from one of the vendor men. Sitting in an old Maruti Omni, he was waiting with bated breath. Another Tempo Traveller was waiting for a call from them to deliver the final fatal blow.

"How long do we have to wait?" Jaani was getting restless after having smoked the eighth beedi under two hours.

"Patience, Jaani, patience. Revenge has never been instantly served. These miserables have destroyed the tranquillity of our lives. They will have to pay the price," Baja was cold and ready. He poured Old Monk rum into his mug and enjoyed it leisurely.

"I hope you have made some arrangements for the night. No sharing tonight," Jaani was sick of the waiting.

"I want blood in my drink today to quench the thirst. Regarding the night, if we get one, I will leave her to you. Don't fret now," Baja was considerate.

"Vehicle number KA 008 ZI 8043," the vendor sent the message that the birds had left the building. Baja was pleased to call the executors and pass the word.

"Another two minutes and we will be done with this mess," Baja was super excited. "These bloody youngsters have messed our business. Now, it is our business to mess up theirs. Cheers!"

He poured rum into Jaani's glass and began pouring the rest of the bottle's contents directly into his throat.

The vehicle numbered KA 008 ZI 8043 passed by their Omni, and Jaani was perplexed to see it. No, he did not have any mercy on Rathishree and Jim, nor were their faces familiar to him. "Baja! It will not work … they are in a Tata Indica and not on a two-wheeler," Jaani screamed. The boss lost control and freaked out under the influence of alcohol. It would derail the purpose. For sure, the Indica had pulled a hundred metres ahead of them, and the Traveller would hit the car after three hundred metres. He took out the mobile and with shaking fingers dialled the number. The mobile network was not reachable at the gravest hour of need. The entrepreneurs drove a bike-on-rent to the venue and returned by hiring a taxi, and thus triggered a change not anticipated by Baja and Jaani.

"Start the car, you bastard!" Baja screamed at Jaani, and by the time they could cover fifty metres, the Traveller had hit the Indica. "You motherfucker, stop the car," and Baja got the Omni stopped two hundred metres before the accident spot. The two victims were severely injured. The shattered windshield injured the rear-row occupants. The crowd was over a hundred in number, somebody dialled for an ambulance and others called the police. Jaani's worst fears came true. Rathishree and Jim were critically wounded, but they were far from dying. Baja applied his mind and said they couldn't take any further risks and be identified. Returning to their Omni, the culprits fled the scene.

The injured victims were admitted to the nearby Apollo Hospital.

The Tempo Traveller as well as the Tata Indica were not doing speeds of greater than twenty-five kilometres per hour. Fortunately, the rear-row occupants were wearing safety belts. Otherwise, the whiplash would have had a severe impact on Rathishree and Jim, and the critical wounds might have become fatal. The accident was a second rear-end collision for the rented taxi. The owner opted for the cheapest windshield as a substitute and not the safer glass. The brunt of that compromise was borne by the occupants at the time of the accident. The shattered glass had made twenty-one lacerations on Jim's and eighteen on Rathi's body. Their faces bore the worst impact.

Veena rushed to the hospital after finding out about the accident from Josh, who in turn had come to know from the joint chat group. Josh was still busy with official work at Goa. The media tried to sensationalize the case yet again, and Jim told them not to scandalize everything. He rationalized that this was as genuine an accident as it could be. The Tempo Traveller driver who hit the rented taxi surrendered to the police. Though they had critical injuries, the scans revealed no fractures at all, and both of them were set to be released the next day itself. Reluctantly, the media left the hospital.

A journalist was bitching that it was the second time in the day that sensationalism was averted in the same case. Veena crossed the media and was pleased to see Jim and Rathi. She mildly remarked that the patches and band-aid strips all over the face made them look a bit cartoonish, and Rathishree laughed and then groaned in pain as her face hurt.

"Sorry, sorry! I didn't mean to rub salt on your wounds," Veena smiled. Rathi was pleased to see the charming lady, and that by itself was a solace for her. Koyal was already present, and the newly engaged couple's parents paid a due visit and were in the familiar visitor's arena.

Rudra stormed in with a bag of cuss words on his lips. He was sure that no matter how generous Rathi and Jim might be, the mafia was undoubtedly behind the accident. In a low tone, he declared that he already knew one of the leading head's mobile number, and he would get back at them. They had to pay the price for killing his friend Sagar and trying to kill Jim and Rathi. He swore not to be a bystander anymore. Rathi did not try to contradict him as she and the team were sure that Rudra meant only empty threats.

After thirty minutes, Veena politely excused herself and said that she had to return home. Rudra stopped her, saying he would also like to join her. He begged her to wait outside for five minutes as he would like to discuss pressing matters with the team. He joined her promptly after twenty-four minutes. Koyal obviously stayed back to be with her fiance. Veena could easily hear Rathi shout in agony, "Don't do anything stupid."

Rudra accompanied Veena and the two walked their way to the parking zone. He had taken a two-wheeler on rent and was surprised to find that Veena drove her own two-wheeler. She said that she left in a hurry on hearing about the accident and hence she took out her bike. He said that he did not have a helmet, and the biker said it was not an issue as two helmets were always locked with her bike. "You mean Activa," he smirked, and she merely nodded in agreement. Walking beside the woman who towered nearly half-a-foot over him, thanks to the heels for sure, he complimented her for being the most charming woman with the most creative brain he had met personally.

When the duo neared the line of parked two-wheelers, Rudra pointed to an Activa and asked if that was hers, and she agreed. A call came in from a familiar friend on the mobile and he received it. He informed the friend that he and Veena were returning home on the latter's Activa. Updating the caller of Jim and Rathi's health, he said he would tell the details after reaching home, as he did not want to keep her waiting. He then turned to Veena who had taken out the two-wheeler and offered him the helmet.

"A sports bike?" he whistled in ecstasy. "Two lakh rupees?"

"Ten. Please sit!" Veena sparked life in the engine and fire in his heart.

What a graceful lady and a smoking hot pie! Veena cut through the traffic like a professional biker of the highest calibre. There was not another biker who could match her on the road. He was totally blown away by the way she controlled the monstrous beast Yamaha MT-09. Her lover Josh drove the Royal Enfield Classic 350, and Rudra too had driven it multiple times. At a signal, he offered to drive the bike, and she categorically ruled it out. She said that even Josh was not allowed to drive her motorcycle, and there was no question of her entertaining him for any and all reasons. He asked her at the next signal if they could stop at a bar for a beer. She said he could get off if badly in need of the beer, but she had to hit home at the earliest. When he tried to say something at the third signal, she promptly asked him to remain quiet. Quiet, and not shut up. She said that it was because she had to mentally think about unknotting a complex code. Thirty-three minutes later, they reached Greenville.

Rudra was in for another surprise when Veena parked the bike at the conventional arena. Taking both the helmets, she locked them with the bike and looking at his surprised eyebrows, she said she had other engagements in the day. When the two entered the lift and Veena pressed the button for their floor, Rudra gave her a quick friendly hug and stopped the elevator doors from closing.

"I badly need my beer, sorry," he winked and stepped out of the lift on his way to the nearby Madhuloka.

Work had been piling up and her focus was letting her down. It had never happened earlier, and she was struggling to rebound from the lapses. Water! She needed to fill her bottle with water. Walking to the kitchen through the hall, she could unmistakably hear a foot tapping in the balcony. Josh was due to return, and it had to be him. Sliding the glass door, a whiff of cigarette smoke hit her nostrils. "Oh, girl!' the voice was disturbing. It was Rudra's.

"What the hell are you doing here? How did you even enter here?" Veena was furious.

"Trespass! Do you think it is possible? With all your security?" Rudra groaned.

"How did you enter here despite the security?" she did not like his presence one bit. The beer and tobacco odour was becoming unbearable.

"Here is the swipe card. You might identify it," Rudra handed her the card belonging to Josh.

"How did you get it?" Veena asked him.

"Your bloody Josh and my whore girlfriend are making out in my very bedroom. Come with me," he started walking out towards his flat.

What was there to think? How was it even happening? Was Josh really in the neighbouring apartment? A million questions were not stopping her from following Rudra. She at least had the sense to carry her own card and her iPhone secured by a pink colored Peppa Pig 3-D embossing mobile cover.

"Find it yourself," he said in a shallow tone as they entered 1304. She walked towards Rudra's bedroom as he was struggling to undo the straps of the sandals, "Barge in!"

The door was ajar, and a dim lamp was lit. Veena entered the bedroom, and the queen-sized bed had wrinkled sheets. Yashu's dress was lying on the floor, and she could hear the shower from the bathroom. The door clanked closed. When she turned around, the dim light was turned off, and there was pitch darkness. She tried to shout, sensing danger, and her vocals betrayed her. She turned again towards the bed with the hope of some mobile rays, or something that might provide the hopelessly required hope and light. Finding nothing, she turned towards the door again.

A hand sneaked between her arm and side chest, curving along the back. Another hand tucked on the small and pulled her in a hug. Much before she realized what was happening, she was being kissed. It was the fastest her lips went inside somebody's mouth. It was the sweetest she was being kissed. Who was kissing her? Certainly not Rudra, who was reeking of tobacco less than a minute ago. The single-piece dress she had slipped in after reaching home to be comfortable was effortlessly taken off her body. Josh was certainly not her kisser. She was now only in her panties. She was struggling to come by, and then she was deeply smooched again. Her kisser soon entered two fingers between her legs and kissed her on the breast, sucking the nipple hard. Tears began rolling down her cheeks.

"No, my lovely Veena. Don't cry, don't break my heart," Yashu saw her dream come true.

Two hours later, Rudra came into the room. He smiled and tried to enter the bed. "Sorry, she is mine only," Yashu was possessive of her prize catch.

Rudra took out his mobile and dialled Jaani's number. He had got it by torturing Alok and accidentally killing him. Three rings later, the call was received with a hello.

"Jaani bhai!" said Rudra. The speaker mode was turned on.

"Wrong number," Jaani's default answer to unknown numbers.

"*PaPi entrepreneur, PaPi*," Rudra screamed to ensure it reached before Jaani could cut off the call. Veena got out of Yashu's embrace.

Jaani thought for a moment, looked at Baja for approval and got it. "PaPi! What's your connection with PaPi?" Jaani asked.

"Look Jaani bhai! I am Sagar Bansal's friend. We are ready to quit the enterprise and shut it down forever. Today, you attacked Rathishree and Jim too. We want all this to stop and leave the online sales business completely. As a final settlement, we are ready to give you ten lakh rupees. Please spare us," Rudra said politely, and then grinned with fury. The neighbour put on her undergarments.

"Ten lakhs? Do you think we are beggars?" Jaani laughed.

"We are not rich people, Jaani bhai. After today's attack, we have decided to exit from your world. Ten lakh rupees is all that we have. Anything more, and you can as well kill us. But please spare us," Rudra begged. The scholar wore her dress and while she fastened to pick her mobile and swipe card, the fore flap got torn and fell about four feet away.

"Finally, you stupid bastards have come to your senses. Two o'clock. Come to the Chandra Layout Indian Oil petrol pump. Dump your money, and leave," Jaani ordered.

"No, we want to give the money to you only," Rudra insisted on a meeting. Veena picked her and Josh's forged swiping cards.

"You take me for a fool. You will then want to hand me over to the police," Jaani laughed.

"Before his death, I tortured your boy Alok. I killed him. Before dying, he not only gave me your mobile number, he gave the perfect sketch of yours. I can hand over that sketch to the police even now. But I want to settle this between us. If you are not there, I will not give a single rupee," Rudra laughed a bit now.

The scholar was back in her safe haven and changed the access codes on the cards. She wept after finding Yashu in place of Rathi. The surprise was being dominated by the five-inches-shorter girl even as the shock element provided the cover. No tears, Veena, no tears.

Rudra and Yashu had a definitive plan. It was near fool-proof. Rudra's confidence stemmed from getting scotfree with Alok's murder. He was just a suspect, just as any engineer/entrepreneur among the millions in Bengaluru. The don was undoubtedly stunned by his little lie of a sketch. The number getting leaked was a shock element to the mafia in the same vein as Yashu taking Veena, thanks to the darkness. He had two hours to decide how to attack Jaani and be done with him for good.

His strategy relied heavily on Yashu's response. He planned to reach the petrol pump exactly at 2 a.m. An hour earlier, he would survey the place and hide Yashu at an apt strategic point. When he would be dealing with Jaani, she would distract everyone by playing a ghost shrieking on her mobile. Jaani would be distracted for five seconds at least, and in that time, he would finish his adversary.

Around twelve-thirty, Rudra and Yashu left HSR Layout on their Vespa Elegante, and according to the strategy, he marked that she could hide behind a barrel. Thank goodness, the attendant was dozing and snoring heavily. Around one-thirty, he left Yashu at the ICICI ATM higher on the cliff. She steadily and confidently walked from the higher altitude to Indian Oil petrol pump and hid behind the barrel. Thirty minutes later, precisely at the scheduled time, he reached the bunk. Jaani was expected anytime.

Five minutes passed by. Ten minutes also completed. Rudra was now getting nervous, Yashu as well. As he looked up the hill on both sides, there was no sign of life. He sauntered towards the barrel.

A sound. A ringtone. Damn it, a call on Yashu's number at the devil's hour. Yashu got up in horror and showed the displayed number on her screen: 'Private Number'. Rudra snatched the mobile and took the call and shouted hello.

"A small change in plan, Rudra," said a machinated voice. "We are waiting on the bridge of the Nagarabhavi pass towards the National Law College, Jnanabharathi."

"Come down here, you bastard Jaani. You agreed to come to the petrol pump," Rudra shouted in despair.

"Ah, the sensitive nerves! Send your little girl Yashashwini first. You start after she reaches here. We want to taste her too. You give the money and take your girl. Don't waste time, and ask her to leave by the count of five. Else, I blow up the petrol pump," the machinated voice laughed.

"I am coming," Yashu agreed, cut the phone, and started walking. She urged Rudra to remain calm. She promised to call him after reaching Jaani over the bridge.

Two minutes passed by; Yashu should be at the top of the high hill. Another minute went by; she must have reached the university road. Suddenly, steps were heard running downwards in his direction. He prayed that it was not the police.

The steps ran inside the bunk, and Rudra was shocked to see... shocked to see Veena Rao, of all the people. She was carrying a bag in her hand.

"Look Rudra, I was hiding in the side lane. I saw Yashu going towards the university. Didn't Jaani turn up here?" Veena asked.

"Veena, what are you doing here at this time of the night?" Rudra was still in disbelief.

"Well, I heard your call with Jaani. I suspected your plan might fail. Remember what Rathi told as we left her, 'Don't do anything stupid?' What you and Yashu planned was stupid. So, I came with ten lakh rupees. In case you can't convince Jaani, I thought it would be useful. Where did she go?" Veena asked.

Rudra's mobile rang, and there was a call from Yashu. As expected, she asked him to start. He started off with Veena and told her the changes as they were walking up the hill.

"She might be in trouble, Rudra. Let us reach her rapidly," Veena said the correct thing to do, and they began to run. As they were running down, Rudra tripped over something and fell down. When he tried to get up, his knees were hurting badly. A few dogs were growling and looked as if they wanted to attack him and Veena. Veena pretended to pick stones from the ground, and that was enough to fend off the dogs. He begged Veena to support him.

Putting his hand over her shoulder for support, he limped his way. As they were nearing the bridge, Yashu walked towards them. An Omni was parked on the deck, with the fender flung fully open. “Rudra…” Yashu said in horror.

“I tripped over, and my knees are badly hurt. It is almost killing me. Did Jaani abuse you?” Rudra enquired. He also told her how Veena had brought ten lakh rupees to save them from Jaani, if the need arose.

She nodded and added, “No, he didn’t. Come with me!” Yashu directed Veena and Rudra towards the Omni car. When they were five metres near the vehicle, Veena and Rudra saw in horror that Jaani and Baja had been killed in the same style as Alok, Tiku Singh, Ghumroo, Dhyan and Mukesh. “What does that mean?” Yashu could not understand who had killed the mafia dons.

“I don’t know, Yashu. I am clueless,” Rudra confessed.

“The same left-handed cuts by the murderer,” Yashu was shocked.

“Or it can be an ambidextrous woman who does not like lesbianism forced on her,” Veena said.

“What do you mean, Veena?” as Rudra completed his remark, a knife pierced Yashu’s left breast, making a similar mark as the earlier murders. Veena stabbed Yashu twice more in the belly.

“You did not trip, Mr Rudra. That was me,” Veena proved with two strong kicks on his weakened knees. Without any doubts, he was now handicapped for life, if Veena did not kill him.

“Stupid girl! She was over-smart in insisting the murderer was a left-hander. You killed Alok and tried to penetrate the mafias, but you did not get the relevant information. Yashu left the cut on Alok first. I know she also killed Tiku Singh, Ghumroo and Dhyan in the same way, and tried to make it look as though